THE HAUNTED HILLS

The grim order tenderfoot Shelton Sherman was given shortly after he took a job at Sunbeam Ranch was simple: "If he comes, shoot!"

But did shooting make sense? Could bullets down a ghost?

While riding in the hills, Sherman had come upon tracks that were neither animal nor human. Then a flock of sheep was killed by having their necks twisted. Days later a sheepman's neck was broken the same way. Terror spread over the entire range. Some ranchers branded Alec Vurney, owner of the Sunbeam and a hater of sheepmen, as the murderer. But that did not explain the weird cries that echoed from the hills or the ugly shape that drifted through the night. Sherman rode to find an explanation. It was a ride that brought him to a monster and close to death!

THE HAUNTED HILLS

B. M. Bower

GUNSMOKE

First published in the UK by Little, Brown

This hardback edition 2006
by BBC Audiobooks Ltd
by arrangement with
Golden West Literary Agency

ISBN 1 4056 8067 9

British Library Cataloguing in Publication Data available.

Printed and bound in Great Britain by
Antony Rowe Ltd., Chippenham, Wiltshire

THE HAUNTED HILLS

CHAPTER ONE

ANOTHER TENDERFOOT

In that part of Idaho which lies south of the Snake River, the land is spotted with forest, sage flats, lava beds and grassland. You can find anything there—anything in the shape of wild desolation. In the days when the Sunbeam held by right of possession the range which lay east and south of the low group of mountainous hills, you could find more of the desolation, more of the forbidding wilderness than the land now holds. The Sunbeam ranch—which includes that stretch of fertile land where stood the Sunbeam buildings—was tucked away in a coulee so hidden that one might ride to the very rim of it before suspecting its nearness.

Idaho is full of such coulees. You ride through miles and miles of bleak desert with nothing to break the monotony save a distant blur of rock-crowned hills. You enter a nest of thickly strewn bowlders, perhaps, and turn and twist this way and that to avoid the biggest. Then you find yourself on the brink of a steep hill—or perhaps a cliff—and just below lies a green little valley with trees and a trout stream; or a gray little valley with sagebrush crowding upon the narrow strip of grass which borders the dry creek bed; or a black hole of a valley that looks like the mouth of hell itself, with gleaming ledges of black lava interspersed with sharp-cornered rocks the size of your head, and stunted sage and greasewood and no water anywhere.

If you go down there, you will hear the buzz of a rattler before you find your way out again, and you will see horned toads scuttling out of sight in little crevasses, and lizards darting over bowlders into some hiding place just beyond. You will see the bluest sky in the whole world arching the barrenness from rim to rim; or perhaps it only seems so

3

blue when it looks down upon so much that is black and utterly desolate.

The Sunbeam cabins stood in one of the gray little valleys. Farther along there was a meadow, to be sure, where hay was cut for the saddle horses to feed upon in winter. But that was around a black elbow of lava, thrust out toward the stream like the crook of a witch's arm hiding jealously the green little nook where lay the meadows. The cabins were built upon barren sand, perhaps because the green places were too precious to be used improvidently for mere comfort in living.

Since every story must begin somewhere, suppose we start with a muggy evening when Shelton C. Sherman arrived at the Sunbeam, convoyed hither by one called Spooky. Shelton C. Sherman had always considered himself much handicapped by his name, over which unaccustomed tongues tripped most irritatingly. He must have owned a stubborn streak, since in spite of his intense dislike he refused to resort to initials only and watched with a secret defiance the reaction of strangers to the name he hated. He was even more sensitive and rebellious because of his good looks, which he hoped to remedy somewhat during the summer by hiding his girlish complexion beneath the thickest coat of tan he could possibly manage to acquire.

Shelton C. Sherman was a tenderfoot and knew it. He had read Bret Harte and Owen Wister and was still undecided as to just what course he had better take if the Sunbeam cowboys tried shooting at his feet to make him dance. He had learned boxing at college long before he ever expected to come west, and he was not unfamiliar with guns, which provided him with a nice problem in retaliation. Should he shoot or should he fight—or should he just go ahead and dance? Being an amiable young man with a fairly well-trained brain, he was rather inclined to wait and see what spirit was shown in the hazing.

Unobtrusively, he studied Spooky beside him and decided not to swallow anything that plausible young cowpuncher told him. At the same time, he must appear to swallow it. That was part of the game. Of course, everyone

4

would lie to him and play tricks on him—he expected that. Which proves how green he really was, for Spooky actually told him the truth about most things.

"You don't want to let Burney put you on the fence, first thing," Spooky coached, when they were within five miles of the ranch. "Burney's all right, once you get to know him right well. You take it from me, there ain't a straighter, whiter man in Idaho than Alec Burney."

"Well, why does he put people on the fence, then? Must be something queer about him." Too conscious of his ignorance, the tenderfoot was on his guard. "I must confess I don't quite get the point."

"Oh, I meant throw a scare into yuh," Spooky explained with patience. "He scares kids until they get used to him. But if you go at him right, you'll soon get to like him."

"How should I go at him?" Shelton laid a hand upon his thigh and lifted a long, lean leg out over the broken dashboard to relieve a cramped muscle. Spooky reserved his reply while he took a more careful inventory of his passenger.

"Say, you sure are all there lengthways, ain't yuh?" he observed with reluctant admiration. "About how high do yuh stack up alongside a hole in the ground, anyway? All of six feet, ain't yuh?"

"Two inches over," Shelton admitted. "The folks sent me out here to get some width to go with my length. Dad's an architect. He said he'd have to use me for a straight edge if I didn't stop growing long and start in widening out pretty soon."

"Unh-hunh. Well, she sure is a great country. I reckon maybe you'll widen out if you stay long enough. How old are yuh?"

"Not as old as I expect to be before I'm through," Shelton evaded good-humoredly. Then he reconsidered. "I'm twenty-one, if it really matters. Time will remedy that, and if it will also put some meat on my bones and take off this pretty-pretty complexion that will make me the butt of all your jokes, I'll be willing to stay ten years."

Such frankness was somewhat disconcerting. Spooky touched up the off horse, which was inclined to "soldier"

5

on the up-grade pull through a stretch of loose sand. "Oh, you'll make out, all right," he said finally. "Us boys ain't as bad as we're painted. Long as you ain't one of them know-it-alls—can you ride?"

"You mean on a horse?"

"I mean—on a horse, yes." Spooky sighed.

"Well, I never was on one except once. I fell off that time," Shelton confessed honestly. "If it was a bike, I've won a good many bicycle races, and fancy trick stuff is my meat." He looked out across the dismal, gray expanse. "That's no good here, of course. Too rough."

Spooky made no reply to that. He drove on for some minutes in deep thought, eyes on the trail.

"Had you anything in particular in mind when you asked me if I could ride a horse?" Shelton C. Sherman prompted, when the silence became marked.

"I was goin' to say you'd brown up when you got out after stock, but I've changed my mind. In order to git tanned and looking more human like, I guess you better set on the corral fence, bareheaded, a couple or three hours a day—'til your nose peels a time or two."

"I'd rather sit on a horse, if it's all the same to you," Shelton objected. "I'm pretty certain I can learn to ride, don't you think?"

"Oh-h—I guess maybe you could." Spooky spoke guardedly. "You're pretty old to start in, but maybe you could learn."

"Gosh! It certainly is a relief to hear I'm too old for something. I've had my extreme youth held over my head until I'm good and sick of it. What do you call that line of hills over there?" He pointed. "I'd like to investigate them some day."

"Them? Us Sunbeamers call them the Haunted Hills. Over there's where—" Spooky stopped, spat over the wheel into the sand and neglected to finish the sentence. He stared morosely at the jagged, black sky line and touched up old Blinker again with the whip more severely than was needful.

"That's rather a peculiar name. Are they supposed to be haunted?"

6

Spooky meditated upon the advisability of answering truthfully. After a space of silence he said seriously, "Well, that's what folks say."

"Well, and what do *you* say about it? Do you know of any spooks over there?"

"Yeah, I do. One, anyway. That's why folks call me Spooky—'cause I seen a spook over there in them hills. D' you believe in 'em?"

Shelton stuck both legs out over the dashboard and stared reflectively at the hills. "Well, I never have," he said simply. "But I expect I could, if I were shown any convincing reason for believing. I came out here into this country prepared to believe almost anything."

Spooky eyed him sidelong, gave a sudden snort, then topped it off with a chuckle. He was not a bad sort, though he was an awful liar when the mood seized him and he could find a pair of credulous ears willing to listen. Again he spat over the wheel, pointed with his whip toward a certain low ridge, blocked at either end by high buttes, and by devious conversational bypaths he proceeded to tell a very creditable ghost story.

"Gosh!" Shelton C. Sherman paid tribute and turned to stare with a new interest at the jagged peaks and gloomy hollows. "I wonder if I could get a sight of it sometime? You say it sank into the ground with a low, pitiful moan?"

Again Spooky squinted at him sidelong. "It went into the ground, yes. But I never said it done any pitiful moanin'. The dang thing hollered so my back hair never laid down for four days."

He went at Blinker with the whip, set him into a gallop, and then sawed the horses into a heavy-footed trot again. "Mebbe you got your doubts about it bein' true," he observed challengingly. "Lemme tell yuh somethin', young feller. You ain't the first to doubt it."

"I'm sure I never intimated that I doubted your word," Shelton protested suavely.

"You don't have to. Me, I'm tone-broke. Spider, he never believed it, either, when I told about it at the ranch. And then, about two months back, Spider, he was prognosticating around over there, trailin' a mountain lion; and *he* heard

7

it. And he was so danged scared he plumb dropped his rifle and come foggin' home without it. That's a fact. You can ask any of the boys. You ask Spider what he seen over in them hills. That's all—you just ask him."

"I shall," Shelton obligingly promised. "I wonder if it would scare me if I saw it."

"Hell!" grunted Spooky. "Don't yuh know?"

"No," Shelton declared. "You see, I've never *been* scared. I was in a train wreck, once—when two elevated trains smashed together—and that didn't scare me, though people around me were yelling and screaming and women were fainting all over the place. And I was in a theater panic another time, and I stood upon a seat and watched the people fighting like wildcats to get to the door, and that didn't scare me, either. I was just interested and sorry for the poor idiots who couldn't keep their heads. And I've been held up and robbed with a gun in my wishbone, and once I was upset in a canoe before I'd learned to swim very well. And I was hazed good and plenty at school, of course—but I never could seem to get scared about it. Not scared like some fellows get, you know, so they drop guns and run, or be so scared folks would call them Spooky ever afterwards. I was just wondering if you really had something out here that would do the work."

Spooky twisted his body around in the seat and looked Shelton C. Sherman over carefully, cold suspicion in his eyes. Shelton took in his legs, gave two perfectly unconscious pulls at his trousers—after the manner of a man who hates baggy knees—and returned the stare with clear-eyed candor.

"I was wondering if that spook thing could scare me," he finished deprecatingly.

"I—Blinker! I'll cut the everlastin' hide offen you, if you don't straighten out them trace chains!"

"Was it the looks of it, or do you think it was the noise that scared you?"

Spooky shifted himself uncomfortably on the seat. "I dunno. I'll take yuh over there some day and let yuh find out for yerself."

"Oh, would you? Thanks!" His tone was so absolutely

8

honest that Spooky withdrew into his shell of taciturnity, and gave over his half-formed plan of mental bedevilment, and drove on in silence, except when common decency wrung from him a yes or a no, or his one safe bet, "I dunno."

He took the young man to the house and left him standing there in the heavy dusk with his baggage stacked beside him and bewilderment in his eyes. The Sunbeam did not run to artistic housing, and it is very probable that the young man experienced a keen sense of dissappointment when he stood before the low, dirt-roofed cabin that sprawled upon a sun-baked area of sand, and realized that this was the official headquarters of the Sunbeam ranch.

Spooky lifted his head and yelled a summons, and a door opened to let out a huge figure that loomed monstrous in the dusk. Spooky went to the head of Blinker and stood there fumbling with the harness, which was his way of masking the watchful stare he fixed upon his passenger. By every line of his figure, Spooky was waiting expectantly, hoping to see some sign of perturbation in this young man who so naïvely professed his ignorance of the sensation of fear.

The gigantic figure came closer and closer until he towered above his visitor; towered, though Shelton had owned to six feet two. Spooky grinned in anticipation and moved closer, pretending to be looping up Blinker's line.

Shelton C. gave one surprised look and went forward, smiling. "Are you Mr. Burney? I'm Shelt Sherman. I think you expected me—unless Mother's letter went astray somewhere."

The giant took the hand of Shelton C. Sherman and half crushed the bones in an excruciating grip. Spooky watched the young man's face—watched and saw him smile wryly, and heard him make the amazing statement that he was awfully pleased to meet Mr. Burney. Under his breath, Spooky named the place where liars must go when they die, and without another look he finished unhitching the team and led them away to the stable.

He met Spider on the way and stopped long enough to announce that he had brought a pilgrim home with him.

"He's a purty-purty and he ain't never been scared in his life, and he ain't never been on a hoss in his life, except once

9

when he didn't stay long, and he laid his trustin' little hand in Burney's and said he was awfully pleased to meet him. Mebbe you c'n read his brand from that. Damned if I can."

"Huh!" said Spider, mentally picturing the pilgrim. "One of these smart alecks, huh? 'S he goin' to stay?"

"You can search me. He sure *thinks* he is." Spooky was stripping the harness off the horses. "He's got a banjo. He ain't so worse. Kind of a friendly cuss. But he sure is tender!"

"He'll get over that," Spider stated wisely. "If he stays long enough, he will."

"Yeah—if. Wonder what Burney wanted him out here fer? Looks like he's got enough on his hands without takin' no kid to raise."

CHAPTER TWO

DO GHOSTS EVER DUCK?

THE CABIN was low and gloomy for want of windows. Burney bent his head level with his chest whenever he entered or left his own door, yet he never thought of building a house to match the hugeness of his frame. Burney was six feet and eleven inches tall when he was barefooted. His cabin was built with a clearance of a little more than seven feet to the ceiling inside; so Burney, desert bred though he was and living most of his life in the outdoors, had the manners of a gentleman in one respect, at least. He never wore his hat in the house. Bareheaded, he did not scrape the ceiling when he walked about, unless he went close to the wall. When he did that, he ducked his head automatically without ever giving it a thought.

Shelton C. Sherman spent the whole of the first evening in watching Burney with something of the amazed incredulity which marks the gaze of a small boy when he sees his first elephant. When Burney rose from his chair—made of planks spiked together so that it formed a square stool which would have borne the weight of a horse—Shelton glanced involuntarily upward to see if Burney were going to crack his head on the pole ceiling. When Burney turned his back, Shelton made mental calculation of the breadth of those shoulders and then refused to believe the figures his mathematical training told him were correct.

Burney sat down before the fire. Shelton stared at the huge boots thrust forward to the heat, half expecting that Burney would presently call out, "Wife, bring me my hen!" And if you have never read the story of Jack the Giant Killer, you will not see any sense in that.

When Burney filled his pipe, Shelton wondered how he managed to avoid crushing the bowl of it in his fingers. He caressed the swollen knuckles of his right hand and stared with astonishment at the light touch of Burney when he picked a coal from the fire and dropped it neatly into the center of the pipe bowl.

There were two things small about Burney. His eyes, which in the firelight looked like little twinkling blue sparks, and his voice, which was pitched rather high, with a light tenor quality which sounded almost womanish. But he seldom spoke. During the entire evening he volunteered only two questions. He asked Shelton how his mother was and half an hour later he inquired concerning Shelton's age.

At the bunk house the boys discussed the newcomer and wondered how he was making out, shut up alone with Burney. Spooky's curiosity led him as far as the window of the cabin. He peeked in, Spider looking over his shoulder. The scene within was disappointing in its tranquillity. Shelton C. Sherman was sitting on an upturned nail keg, smoking a pipe and staring meditatively into the fire. While they watched him, he removed the pipe to crowd down the filling and yawn widely as he did so. Three feet away, Burney sat upon his plank stool with his great made-to-order riding boots thrust away out toward the blaze, also smoking his pipe and staring mediatively into the fire.

Spider craned for a good look at the pilgrim, saw him lift his right hand after a quiet moment and run the finger tips of his left hand gingerly over the swollen knuckles. He glanced afterward at Burney with a quiet look of inquiry, and Spider snickered and nudged Spooky in the ribs.

"Looka that?" he whispered. "I betcha he carries that paw of his in a sling to-morrow."

"Reckon he'd like to, all right—but he shore stood for it like a little major, and said he was pleased to meet him,"

11

Spooky whispered back, reluctantly giving credit where credit is due.

"Huh!" murmured Spider, and led the way back to the bunk house.

Breed Jim was there, just having put up his horse after a late ride from over toward Pillar Butte. That in itself was not far enough out of the ordinary to merit a thought. But the look on Breed Jim's face as he glanced up at the two caught their attention and drew their speech away from the visitor.

"Say," Jim began, without prelude of any sort, "where was it you seen that there ghost of yourn, Spooky?"

"Ghost uh mine? I ain't payin' taxes on no ghost," Spooky denied indignantly. "What you driving at, anyhow? Come in at this time uh night and begin on me about—"

"I ain't beginnin' on nobody." Jim pried off the corner of a fresh plug of tobacco and spoke around the lump. "I seen something out on the aidge of the lava bed. Follered me for about a mile. I couldn't ride away from it and I couldn't get within shootin' distance. It was too dark to make out what the thing was—but it shore as hell was *something*. Scared my horse so I couldn't hold him, hardly."

"Whereabouts on the lava bed?" Spider wanted to know. "Up next the hills? That's where I seen something last winter."

"No, not up there. I was away over on the fur side uh that black coulee. You know the one I mean—heads up into the big butte. I hit the coulee just about dusk (she got dark quick tonight) and I was driftin' along toward the Injun trail to get across the coulee and come on home, when I first felt the thing follering."

"Felt—?"

"Yeah, by gosh, I *felt* it. Somethin' kinda told me I was bein' follered and I commenced lookin' back. First time or two I didn't see nothing. I was comin' along through the rocks and if they'd been a hull army uh soldiers I couldn't uh seen 'em. I went on a little piece further and looked back again; and I never seen nothin' that time, neither. But I knowed damn well there *was* something—I could feel my back crawl cold, kinda."

"One of these here imaginary spooks, huh?"

"Not on your life. I knowed there was something, and more'n all that, my horse got to actin' oneasy like, and he kept lookin' back. Horses don't do that just for a feller's imagination. It went along like that until I come to the Injun trail, and then I seen something back a piece behind me, just duckin' behind a big rock."

"Do ghosts ever duck?" Shelton C. Sherman was standing by the half-open door, listening to the talk. Now that he had spoken, he entered the room, his hat in his hand. Seen in the yellow lamplight, his face was positively angelic.

"Pardon me for seeming to eavesdrop," he said, in his pleasant, friendly voice. "I didn't mean to, but I arrived just at the point where your back crawled cold. That sounded so intcresting, I waited to hear the rest of it. Sherman is my name, fellows. Shelton C. Sherman, and you needn't try to say it all when you're in a hurry. I'm just as green as they make them in stories; possibly a shade greener than any you've read about. But Mr. Burney sent me down here to sleep, so I've just about got to force myself upon you and crawl into some corner where I won't be too awfully conspicuous."

He grinned down at Jim with that cheerful candor which Spooky had found so disarming. "Won't you please go on with your story?" he begged. "I didn't mean to interrupt, honest. But I was so interested, I forgot my manners."

"Huh!" Jim grunted from behind the mask of stolidity which he wore for strangers and comforted himself with more tobacco. He made no attempt to go on with his story, however.

"This is only the young feller I brung out from town," Spooky explained. "Burney's took him to raise; calls himself Shep for short—or somethin' like that. You don't have to mind him, Jim. Go ahead and tell us."

"Yeah, what did he look like? A man?" Spider sat down on the end of a bunk and leaned forward with both elbows resting upon his knees.

Jim shook his head, sending a quick glance at Shelton from under his black eyebrows. "I dunno what it was like."

"Didn't yuh see it again?"

"Nh-hn!" Jim got up, went to the door and looked out,

13

mumbled something about his horse, and disappeared into the night.

"Oh, say! I'm afraid I spoiled the whole story," Shelton exclaimed remorsefully. "I didn't mean to do that. What was it all about, anyway? Did he really see something?"

"You can search me," Spooky rebuffed him. "You can sleep in that bunk over there, Shep. Nobody lays any claim to it. The feller that owned it blowed his brains out right in that there bed last fall. Spattered 'em all over the piller."

"That's too bad," Shelton remarked with perfunctory sympathy, and turned the pillow over, inspecting it with care. "He couldn't have had many brains—he certainly didn't leave many signs on the pillow. I never slept with any one's brains but my own before." He looked up at them with a grin. "I certainly hope I don't dream double tonight."

"Well, I'll be damned!" Spider murmured under his breath, and shook his head with a helpless gesture.

Shelton glanced at him inquiringly. "Oh, don't think I mind. I don't, at all. I'm tired enough to sleep any old place. I hope you don't bother about my comfort—I'll be all right."

"We ain't botherin' about you, Shep," Spooky grinned deceitfully. "Not a damn bit."

He watched covertly while Shelton C. Sherman brought in his suit cases, opened them, displaying an amazing number of carefully folded shirts and underclothes, took out a white linen nightshirt and robed himself in it in the matter-of-fact manner of one who had done that every night of his life.

Spooky sent a meaning glance toward Spider when the nightshirt appeared, and Spider pulled down the corners of his mouth by way of reply to the glance. They watched while Shelton turned back the blankets, inspected them for blood and brains and finally crawled in between them with a long sigh of animal comfort.

Spooky lifted his eyebrows at that. Shelton's apparent indifference to the gruesome history of that bed filled him with suspicion. He picked up a deck of cards, absently shuffled them and made a spread for that game of solitaire which he called Mex.

"You don't want to git to dreamin' about poor old Mike," he warned Shelton, by way of reopening the subject. "The

14

only feller that's tried to sleep there after it happened woke us all up, screamin' and fightin' the air. He was foamin' at the mouth something fierce by the time we got the lamp lit. Took four of us to hold him down. I dunno what got ahold of him—he wouldn't talk about it. We couldn't get a word outa him. But next day he blowed *his* brains out." He glanced sidelong at Spider for the grin of approval he felt that he had earned.

Shelton C. Sherman yawned widely and with unmistakable sincerity and turned over on his back.

"Say, you fellows out here must have all kinds of brains to waste," he made sleepy comment and yawned again, showing two rows of very white, even teeth. "This cabin certainly seems to have a very brainy atmosphere; maybe I'll—absorb some—if I sleep—" he trailed off into a mumble, as his heavy lids dropped and laid a smudge of long, curling lashes upon the delicate pink of his cheeks.

Spooky watched him dumbly, his mouth half open. Presently that thick fringe of lashes lifted and sleepy eyes looked forth. "Good night, fellows," Shelton muttered. "Hit me a punch if I—bother you with—sn-oring." And with that he went to sleep in earnest, his breathing as deep and quiet as if he hadn't a care in the world.

Spooky played in silence until the game was hopelessly blocked. He dropped the remainder of the deck upon the table, got up, took the lamp and went over and held the light close to the sleep-locked eyes of Shelton C. Sherman. He waved the lamp back and forth twice, saw the sleeper move restlessly away from the glare without waking, stood up and looked at Spider. "I'm a son of a gun!" he stated flatly. "Whadda yuh know about a kid like that?"

CHAPTER THREE

"THEY'RE BACK, ALL RIGHT"

Breed Jim went into the cabin where Burney still bulked before the dying embers, his pipe held loosely in his great fingers, his little blue eyes fixed abstractedly upon the filming coals. Jim went over and leaned an elbow on the rough

15

mantle. The Indian gift of silence was in his nature, and it was strong enough to induce a certain deliberateness in beginning what he had come to say. For some moments he stared down reflectively into the fire in brooding silence.

There was no Indian blood in Burney, yet he sat for perhaps five minutes before he stirred so much as a finger. At last he shifted his feet with a scuffing sound upon the rough floor, gave a great sigh as if he were dismissing thoughts somber and burdensome, and looked up.

"Well, what did you find out, Jim?"

"They're back, all right," Jim said, without removing his gaze from the fire. "Been back a month or so. They're runnin' three big bands—mostly ewes. Lambin's on full blast.

"They ain't worked over this side Pillar Butte, yet, but they're grazin' them this way, all right. Feed ain't so good over there and they got to cover lots of ground. They'll be crowdin' up on us, pretty soon."

"Talk with any of 'em?"

"Nh-hn. I kept back on the ridges outa sight and sized things up. I'm pretty sure none of the bunch spotted me. I didn't know what you might want to do about 'em, so I left the game plumb open."

Burney got up and stretched his arms out full length from his body—only in the open could he lift them above his head as he might have liked to do. He had a most amazing reach for any human being outside of a circus, and even under his coat one could see the great muscles flex and swell upon his shoulders.

"They needn't think I'll buy 'em out again," he remarked, half to himself. "I might be a fool, all right, but I ain't a fool twice in the same place."

Jim grinned appreciatively. "They sure as hell made good money offen you last time," he twitted tactlessly. "I dunno as you c'n blame 'em much for bringin' in another outfit to try an' unload on yuh. I guess they made more offen that deal than what you done."

Burney turned and scowled down at him and Jim pulled the grin from his lips and backed up a step. Sometimes Burney would stand for joshing, Jim remembered nervously, and sometimes he wouldn't; and when he wouldn't, silence

16

was a man's best friend.

He waited a minute or so longer, decided that Burney was not going to say anything more—or that if he did speak, what he said would not be pleasant to hear—and left the cabin without a word of explanation or adieu.

Burney walked twice the length of the cabin, hesitated, and opened a door in the end wall; a door so low that he went through it in a crouching position. For some moments he busied himself there in his little storeroom and came out with a bundle under his arm.

He went outside, stood for some minutes upon the doorstep, gazing down toward the bunk house. When he saw the lighted square of the window go dark and open its eye no more, he moved away toward the stable. For all his bulk, he moved swiftly and quietly. From a little distance he would have been no more than a vague shadow drifting through the yard.

In the corral, a big, brown horse nickered softly and came toward the gate, head lifted expectantly. Burney reached out a hamlike paw and the horse nuzzled it like a pet dog. He went over to where his saddle, a huge thing made on a special tree built to his order, hung by one stirrup from the end of a top rail. He did not speak once to the horse that followed at his shoulder, nor while he put on the saddle and the bridle —yet every touch of his hand was gentle and affectionate.

Presently he mounted and rode quietly away through the sagebrush, across the little flat and up the steep hill to the eastward. In the starlight, he looked like the magnified shadow of a horseman moving slowly up toward the stars. Frequently he stopped to breathe his mount; for although the horse was big like his master, and heavy-boned, with deep chest and strong, smooth-working muscles, the hill was steep and Burney was a load for him.

At the top he turned and rode forward on the trail which Breed Jim had lately followed, going at a slow, easy trot that slid the miles behind him with the least possible effort.

Back at the Sunbeam the men slept heavily in the stuffy darkness of the bunkhouse. But Burney, their boss, rode and rode through the sage and the lava, crossed steep gullies and skirted ledges—and still he went on.

17

The Great Dipper tilted more and more and the wind rose and blew chill across the uplands. A thin rind of moon rose and slid behind a flock of woolly clouds that reminded Burney disagreeably of sheep; and after a while the wind grew tired and blew in long, sighing gusts, and then forgot to blow at all. And still Burney was in the saddle, riding alone, with no trail to guide him, and yet with a steady purpose that sent him boring into the night.

When the dawn wind blew chill across the upper reaches, telling that daylight was close behind the deeper gloom of the fading stars, he rode slowly back down the hill and across the barren flat, and stopped at the corral gate.

In the dark he hunted for an old gunny sack in the grain shed, making no more noise than a questing rat. When he had found the thing he was seeking, he unsaddled the big, brown horse and with the sack he rubbed and rubbed until he felt certain that the animal betrayed no sign of having been ridden that night. Then he wiped off saddle and bridle, hung them back upon the rail end (being careful to have horn and headstall turned just as they had been the evening before), closed the gate and went up to the cabin and got into bed.

In the bunkhouse, Spider and Jim and Spooky were sleeping still, with an occasional snort of mumble of half-formed words to show that Spooky was dreaming again. Shelton C. Sherman snored rhythmically on the bed of horrible history. And then the window brightened with the first flush of dawn and the Sunbeam ranch awoke to face the beginning of a new era of its intimate personal history.

CHAPTER FOUR

"YOU'LL COME HOME BY LIGHTNING"

IT TOOK Shelton C. Sherman a week or more to accustom himself to Sunbeam ways, and to the giant Burney, and to the blunt "joshing" of the cowpunchers who called Burney their boss. He learned to accept their sudden disappearances, their unexplained absences and their unexpected arrivals as routine of a cattle ranch. What they did remained pretty much a mystery to him, though he had visions of great herds

18

of cattle being driven from place to place; to new pastures, he guessed—or perhaps to water.

He also learned to accept Burney as a reality and gradually dismissed the fantastic notion that the giant was part of some fairy tale projected into the sage country and likely to turn man-eater at a moment's notice. He learned to answer when some one shouted for "Shep"—for that was the way they twisted his self-confessed nickname of Shelt. In fact, he rather liked the new name. He felt that the cowboys liked him or they wouldn't bother to call him anything at all.

He learned that he must not believe all that they told him, however serious might be their tones and their countenances. The more serious they looked and acted, the less he dared believe. He learned to look for a slyly lowered eyelid and to recognize that particular muscular contraction as a warning signal, and to doubt whatever assertion the winker might make thereafter.

As a matter of fact, he learned a good many things. And since he was young and of a humorous temperament, with a love of all cheerful diversions, he learned much faster than one might suppose. In a week he acquired a doubtful smile and a look of inquiry; in two weeks he had foresworn all faith in his fellows and refused to believe anything he was told; which was almost as bad in its way as was his earlier tendency to believe too much.

Burney drove the first nail into the coffin of his faith and he did it the first forenoon of Shelton's sojourn at the Sunbeam. He found Shelton hanging blankets and quilts on the sagging barbed-wire fence that enclosed a forlorn and barren garden spot. He stood and watched the young man examine a calico-covered pillow.

"What's wrong with that?" Burney asked, in his surprising treble. "We don't throw on much dog around here, but we're clean. You couldn't find a louse in that hull bunk house."

"Why, I'm sure I couldn't. I wouldn't know one of the animals if I should see it," Shelton replied, with his cheerful grin. "I wasn't looking for anything like that. The fellows seemed to think the bedding hadn't been thoroughly cleaned after that man had committed suicide in bed, so I thought

19

it might be a good idea to give these blankets a thorough airing. Not that I'm squeamish—I just thought it would be healthier, maybe. They told me it was on this pillow he blew out his brains—"

"They were just tryin' to run a whizzer on you," Burney stated flatly. "Nobody ever died on this ranch, yet."

Shelton dropped the pillow and stared up at the giant, eyes wide open and lips slightly parted.

"Oh, you mean they lied to me?"

"Sure, they lied to you." A semblance of a smile flickered across his stern mouth. "If anything like that had happened, you couldn't get that bunch within forty rod of the bunk house."

"I don't see why they'd want to tell me a thing like that; do you?" Shelton looked crestfallen.

"They was tryin' to scare you, I s'pose. They wanted to see how you'd take it. What did you do about it?"

"Why," Shelton answered simply, "I didn't do anything about it. There wasn't any other bed available, so far as I could see, so I just went to bed there and went to sleep. Of course, I meant to air the bedding to-day, though."

Burney's little eyes squinted almost shut and his mouth puckered, which was his way of showing amusement. "I guess that's one of them, all right," he made dry comment.

Shelton looked undecidedly at the flapping blankets, then began to pull them off the fence.

"I suppose they'd consider it a great joke on me if they came back and saw all this bedding on the fence," he explained, answering Burney's questioning gaze. "I think I'd better put it back on the bed and wait for their next move. It wouldn't do at all to inform them of the fact that I know they lied, would it?"

"I s'pose they'd lie all the harder, tryin' to prove they told the truth."

Shelton's candid blue eyes studied the big man, almost as if he were trying to decide how much to believe now. Then his thoughts took another turn.

"You really think they did it to scare me?"

"Chances are," Burney answered dispassionately and went on into the cabin.

From that day faith died quickly. Shelton C. Sherman became an extremely distrustful young man who demanded absolute proof before he would accept any statement made to him.

You can see how that would work out in a country where everything was strange, and where ignorance must perforce be warned of many dangers, or suffer the penalty and learn by experience.

"What do you call those hills over there, Mr. Burney?" he asked the giant guilefully one day, and pointed toward the east.

"Them?" Burney turned his head slowly toward the high, broken ridge standing stark and barren against the sky. "Them's the Piute Hills over there."

"The fellows told me they were called the Haunted Hills," said Shelton, in the tone of one who has once again suffered disillusionment.

"They may call 'em that," said Burney, "but that ain't saying it's their name."

"Spooky says he saw a ghost over there."

"Ed's always seein' things."

"I'd like to ride over there, if you don't want me for anything." Shelton was beginning to find little duties around the place, which gave him a satisfying feeling of being one of the outfit, and a lively sense of responsibility. "Could I take old Dutch and a little lunch and do a little exploring to-day?"

"There ain't nothing over there," Burney said, with a shade too much of emphasis. "Why don't you ride over to the river, if you want to go somewhere?"

"I'd rather go to those hills, if it's all the same to you," Shelton persisted. "I've heard so much about them—"

Burney scowled down at him. "You'd git lost."

"Oh, no, I won't. I've got a compass." And Shelton produced a compass the size of a dollar watch and dangled it by its buckskin string before Burney.

Burney snorted at the sight of it. *"That* thing! It'll tell you which way is north, maybe, but it won't tell you when you come to a cañon you can't cross, nor which way you've got to ride to git around it."

"Oh, I leave all those things to Dutch." Shelton smiled

21

disarmingly. "Ought I to take water along to drink or are there streams and springs?"

He tilted back his head and looked up into Burney's face, and the smile faded from his lips. "Why don't you want me to go?" he asked, in the straightforward manner of his which was so disconcerting to the bunkhouse fraternity. "Don't you want me to use old Dutch? You told me I could ride him whenever I wanted to, so I sort of took it for granted I wouldn't need to ask every time."

"Oh, I don't care how much you ride him." Burney was plainly ill at ease.

"Then why don't you want me to ride over that way?"

"Oh, I don't care. Go on and ride where you want to. Only —there ain't anything in them hills to see." Burney pulled out his pipe and began to fill it, his big fingers fumbling over the task.

"Well, maybe I'll see Spooky's ghost," laughed Shelton, and stopped short when he looked up at Burney.

"Ed's a fool," Burney spoke gruffly. "There ain't any such a thing." He spilled tobacco into the wrinkles of his ill-fitting vest.

"Well, but you don't mind if I go and take a look around, do you?"

Shelton did not attempt to understand this big man. He looked so different from other men that one could not expect him to act like others, he reflected. In the week of their acquaintance, he had observed many peculiar traits in Burney. For one thing, he sometimes slept for hours during the middle of the day. To one who did not know him, that would look terribly lazy and shiftless, but Shelton knew that he was neither. Furthermore, he frequently had long fits of silence, during which he seemed morose and sullen, and afterwards he would be querulous with the men so that at such times they avoided him as the simplest means of dodging trouble. Shelton thought that Burney was in one of his unpleasant moods this morning.

"You can do as you please about it, I reckon." Burney spoke even that qualified consent grudgingly.

But it was enough. Shelton took long steps to the stable, having glimpsed Spooky there. He wanted Spooky to help

22

him get the saddle and bridle on Dutch, the proper tying of a latigo being still a baffling mystery to him; also, he could not for the life of him tell which was supposed to be the front of the bridle.

He went grinning up to Spooky and clapped that individual on the shoulder. "I'm going spook hunting," he announced gleefully. "Want to go along?"

"No, I don't want to go along," Spooky retorted, mimicking Shelton's tone. "Spooks don't travel by daylight, Shep. You better wait till towards night before yuh start."

"But I'm going to stay till night," Shelton told him calmly. "I'll take a lunch along. And I've got a compass, so I can come home by the North Star."

"You'll want to come home by lightning if you hear that thing I heard," Spooky fleered. "Wait till you git out in them lava hills and it commences to git darkish! Seems like that's the worst time uh day or night to hit the lava in. All the rocks take on funny shapes—when it gits right dark, you can't see half so much to git skeered at."

"Well, I certainly mean to stay until dark, then. Seems to me it's a funny spook, though, that doesn't wait till midnight."

Spooky's face sobered. He turned a quid of tobacco to the other cheek. "Kinda looks to me like you think we just been kidding you about them hills. Honest to gollies, Shep, they *is* something out there! I wasn't lying to yuh about that."

"You weren't, really?"

"No, by gosh, I wasn't. They's three of us now that saw it and heard it. It ain't human and it shore ain't no animal. It—say, I'll bet four bits you'll come foggin' home with your ears laid back, scairt plumb simple. If yuh come. You wouldn't git *me* out there after sundown—not for this hull ranch and outfit."

"Say, that sounds interesting!" Shelton declared, trying to put the chin strap over old Dutch's nose and wondering what was the matter. "Maybe I'll have something to write home to the folks about. Whoa, old boy! Open your mouth like a good sport."

With an air of weary tolerance, Spooky came up and took the bridle away from Shelton.

23

"Chances are *we'll* do the writin' home to your folks," he predicted ominously, as he slipped the bridle deftly on the horse in the way it was meant to go. "It's all damn foolishness, you goin' prognosticatin' over in them hills. You better keep away from there—and that's straight goods, Shep," he added seriously. "On the dead, it ain't no place for a man to go prowling around alone unless he's got to do it."

"That's just the kind of place I've been looking for. I'm tired to death of nice, safe places that you can pet. I came out here to be real wild and woolly, and Haunted Hills keep a-calling, and it's there that I would be—hunting ghosts that scare our Spooky soon as it's too dark to see!"

He sang the paraphrase of Mandalay, and like the cheerful young reprobate that he was, he went blandly around to the "Injun" side of Dutch and would have climbed into the saddle if Spooky had not grabbed him by the slack of the pants and yanked him back.

"Learn to git onto a horse right, why don't yuh?" the cowboy protested disgustedly. "Mebbe you can't insult poor old Dutch by mountin' like a squaw, but if ever you tackle a real horse that way, you're liable to get your head kicked off."

He watched Shelton go bobbing up the hill and out of sight over the rim, and his eyes were friendly even while he made disparaging remarks about the young man's horsemanship. He liked Shelton C. Sherman with a patronizing, tolerant kind of affection, even though he did lie to him and tease him and bully him outrageously. There was real worry in his eyes and he had half a mind to go after him. But he did not.

CHAPTER FIVE

A RATTLESNAKE PARTY

SHELTON RODE joyously on his way through pungent sage and over hot, barren spaces where nothing moved except the lizards. Spooky had been human enough to give him some really good advice about riding alone. Part of it was to let Dutch use his own judgment and take his own pace in rough country; for Dutch had grown old in the sagebrush, and he was wise with the wisdom of range cayuses. Therefore, having headed for the Haunted Hills, Shelton left the rest to Dutch and rode with his mind at ease.

Barrenness he found, and heat and desolation; and a certain eerie grandeur such as he had never dreamed the land could compass. He did not find anything ghostly about the place, however, and he was disappointed at the prospect of an uneventful day in a wilderness where he had fully expected bold adventure.

He was hot, and the canteen he carried dried on the outside and let the water inside turn warm and brackish. He did not feel like eating the coarse sandwiches of sour-dough bread and cold bacon, and there did not seem to be any place where he could make Dutch comfortable while he rested himself in the shade of a black ledge.

He shot a jackrabbit at forty paces with his nice, new thirty-eight revolver, and was astonished to find himself spread-eagling into a sandy space between two thick clumps of sage. It had never occurred to Shelton that Dutch might object to the sudden report of a gun discharged behind his ears.

Shelton got up and dug sand out of his collar, picked up his hat and laughed sheepishly at the joke he had played upon himself. He led Dutch to where the rabbit lay kicking in the hot sand. It cried like a frightened baby when he drew near and Shelton felt his own throat tighten with the pity of it. A shoulder was broken, and the rabbit's heart thumped so hard that its whole body vibrated with the beating; and when Shelton picked it up and stroked it as one strokes the back of a kitten, its eyes fairly popped with fear.

He spent ten minutes in bandaging the shoulder with his necktie, and while he worked, he talked soothingly to the terrified little animal. He did not want to leave it there in the desert to die, and he could not bear to kill it after the way it had cried. So he held it in the crook of one arm while he mounted awkwardly and rode on, wondering if he could find a cool, shady little nook where the rabbit could stay until its shoulder had healed.

After a long while he thought he heard some one shooting and he turned that way. Not the vicious crack of a large-

25

caliber gun, but the pop of a twenty-two, he thought it was. It must be one of the boys, and yet he could not remember having seen a twenty-two rifle anywhere about the place. He had to grin when he pictured Spooky or Breed Jim riding out into these hills with a gun like that.

Presently he rode out from a huddle of great, black bowlders and heard the rifle crack just beyond the next heap of rocks. He turned that way and came upon a girl sitting at ease upon a flat rock that was shaded by the ledge at her back, staring out across a narrow gulch that was a mere rocky gash in the hill.

While he stared, she lifted her small rifle, aimed carefully with her elbow resting upon a convenient outthrust of the ledge, and fired. She lowered the rifle and peered sharply, aimed and fired again. Shelton looked, but he couldn't, for the life of him, see what she was shooting at.

Dutch snorted and backed. The girl glanced that way and saw Shelton staring curiously, the wounded rabbit held close under one arm.

"Hello!" she said, and turned her attention again to the gulch. Without spilling the rabbit, Shelton managed to dismount, drop the reins to the ground as Spooky had told him he must do, and came forward with his best making-friends manner. Secretly he was a bit disappointed in the girl because her beauty did not go to his head like some rare, old wine. He had read so many Western stories that he had become imbued with the idea that all range-bred girls are entrancingly lovely—romantic heroines waiting to be discovered by the hero of the story. At first glance this girl was not true to type—granting that the story girls are typical. Her hair was a sunburned brown, with neither luster nor sheen; the desert wind saw to that. It seemed abundant enough for any heroine, however, and all native to her own head. She wore it braided and hanging down her back, with the end of the braid falling loosely into two wind-roughened curls. There was no ribbon bow, but a twist or two of what looked suspiciously like common grocery twine. No heroine in any story that Shelton had ever read used grocery twine to tie her hair.

She wore an old felt hat that looked as though it had seen hard usage and a faded calico shirtwaist with a skirt of brown

26

denim. Her face was sunburned with a tendency toward freckles across her nose, and her hands were brown and rough. Little, though, with slender, pointed fingers; and her nails, he noticed, while trimmed close, were immaculately clean.

For the rest, her eyes were a clear blue-gray of the kind that will change color with changing moods and in different lights. No harsh climate nor even primitive living could spoil her mouth, or make it less than beautiful. Red with the clean blood beneath it, finely shaped and sensitive, curving easily into a smile and yet too often drooping into sadness, he thought.

Shelton removed his hat with his free hand and smiled down at her. "How-de-do? What're you shooting at, if I may ask?"

"Rattlesnakes. Better put on your hat; you want to get sun-struck?" The girl glanced briefly up at him again, then aimed and fired once more across the gulch.

"Oh, say! Are you really shooting rattlesnakes? My name is Sherman. Shelton C. Sherman, through no fault of my own. I'm staying at the Sunbeam ranch. You don't mind if I stop a few minutes and watch, do you? It's horribly lonesome in these hills."

"Do you suppose I don't know that?" The girl moved aside to make room for him in the shade and Shelton accepted the mute invitation and sat down beside her. "I guess I know more about lonesomeness than anybody in Idaho. I'm very glad to meet you, Mr. Sherman. In fact, I'm tickled to death to see somebody that doesn't smell of sheep."

Shelton turned and looked at her as long as he dared. "That's awfully good of you," he murmured diffidently.

"No, it isn't. It's just human of me. I have to live right in the middle of a big band. I hear sheep, smell sheep and see sheep twenty-four hours a day, except when I saddle up and get out like this for a while. And then the emptiness and the silence are almost worse than their infernal blatting." Her mouth drooped a little. "I go back to the wagon at night actually somesick for the sheep and the dogs—just because they're something alive." She gave a short laugh. "If that isn't the last word in lonesomeness, I don't know what is."

27

"It certainly does sound like a dreary life for a girl, unless you're just kidding me, the way the boys at the ranch do."

"I only wish I were." The girl stared off across the gulch.

"I didn't know there was a sheep ranch so close," Shelton said, by way of keeping the conversation running along. "Though now I think of it, I have heard the fellows at the Sunbeam talking about some sheep."

"There isn't any ranch," the girl told him brusquely. "I could stand that, because then I'd have a cabin of some kind to take care of. This way, I live in a sheep wagon with Poppy and Uncle Jake. I do the cooking and that's all there is to do. You can't," she explained apathetically, "do much house-keeping in the sheep wagon."

In the past week Shelton had learned to conceal his ignorance whenever it was possible. So now he merely shook his head, and said it did seem rather discouraging to try to keep house in a sheep wagon, though he had not the faintest idea of what a sheep wagon looked like.

"There's another snake!" she announced suddenly, lifting her little rifle. "There must be a regular den over there. I've seen six already. I got four, I think."

She fired and a tiny plop of rock dust shot up into the sunlight and told where the bullet had struck. "Missed," she said indifferently.

"Where is he? I think I'll have a whack at him, myself." Shelton laid down the rabbit, which was too paralyzed with fear to move. "I haven't practised any since I came to the ranch," he explained apologetically. "I've always heard what fine shots the cowboys are and I didn't want them laughing at me. But—"

"But my sample of shooting encourages you to go ahead," finished the girl laconically. "Cowboys don't shoot any better than anybody else," she went on disparagingly. "It's just the name of it they've got.

"Why don't you shoot? Can't you see the snake on the ledge just under where I hit? Looks like a crooked stick. There! Now when he quits crawling, you aim right at his head." She gave a dry, little laugh. "If you can take his head off with *that* gun from over here, you needn't be afraid to shoot before anybody."

28

"Oh, say!" Shelton waited long enough to hug himself clownishly. "This is going to be real Wild West sport! Gee! Shooting rattlesnakes in their dens—"

"Well, shoot first and talk about it afterwards," the girl advised bluntly. "He'll crawl out of sight in a minute."

Shelton obediently raised his revolver high, brought it down in line and fired. The girl watched him curiously now that his attention was diverted from herself. Thus she did not see whether he hit the snake or not and jumped when he gave a whoop.

"Say, am I the lucky child! Did you see him wriggle? Stirred up the whole family too! Gee, look at 'em over there!"

For some moments after that the two were much too busy to talk. Shelton had indeed stirred up the den. Side by side they stood and shot rattlesnakes. When the squirming mass had thinned and quieted down, they sat on the rock in the shade and talked, watching the den and firing whenever a snake showed itself. They had become very well acquainted when the girl got reluctantly to her feet and announced that she must go, or Poppy would wonder where his supper was coming from.

Having learned that one pinched the rattles off the snakes one killed and kept them for souvenirs—in this case for proof of the killing—Shelton insisted upon climbing down into the gulch and collecting all he could find. The girl protested and pointed out the danger in vain. Shelton must have rattles to send to the folks at home as evidence of the truth of the snake story he meant to write. He came back with his nose wrinkled at the overpowering odor down in that hot gulch and looking rather sick; but he had a handful of rattles which he insisted upon dividing with her.

"Oh, say!" he began abruptly, when the division had been accomplished, "you haven't told me your name, yet. I really need to know it, you see. I don't want to keep thinking of you as that girl I shot snakes with."

She turned and looked up at him oddly, a deeper color showing beneath the tan on her cheeks. "You'd laugh," she said, "and I'd probably hate you for it."

"Laugh at a name? When I'm saddled with Shelton C. Sherman—and the C. standing for Clarence, only you mustn't
29

breathe that to a soul. They call me Shep at the Sunbeam."

"Well, mine's Vida; Vidia, really, only I won't stand for that. My mother got it out of the dictionary. It's the feminine of David. I ought to have been a boy, so grandfather could have a child named after him. But I wasn't, so Mother just did the best she could."

"Why, I think that's a beautiful name," Shelton declared, in all sincerity. Then he gave her the wounded rabbit to keep, although she pessimistically assured him that the dogs would kill it the first chance they got, and that if they didn't, it would die of the broken shoulder. But she carried it home with her, nevertheless.

Riding home in the early dusk, it occurred to him that he had forgotten all about the spook. It would have been a good story to tell Vida, only they had seemed to have plenty to talk about without that. He remembered now that she had once spoken of the place as Piute Hills, so she couldn't have heard the spook story. He would tell her next time, sure. He knew she was not the kind of person who believes in ghosts, so it wouldn't scare her. Then he sighed.

She seemed to be an awfully nice girl, though it did seem a shame that she was not as beautiful as the girls he had read about in books. Still, he supposed this was simply the reality he was facing. Let a poet meet Vida and he would find all kinds of things to write poetry about. Her eyes and those long eyelashes, for instance, and her mouth. He supposed that even a famous beauty would get sunburned out in this country unless she wore a veil all the time. And she certainly would have to tie her hair with grocery twine when she ran out of ribbons. So, lost in pleasant musings, he let Dutch find the way home.

CHAPTER SIX

NO ONE COULD SAY IT—SOBER

Spooky had been to town and had returned with the mail, a fresh supply of tobacco and a quart bottle of a liquid which he called a pain-killer. It had been full when he started for the ranch. When he arrived it still was a good three quarters full. This condition the other boys speedily changed until the bottle was thrown into the discard, empty and therefore useless.

Thus it transpired that by dark the Sunbeam boys were jollier than usual and quicker to see a joke—especially when the joke was on the other fellow. When Spooky remembered the mail and took a bundle of letters from his pocket, the number of those addressed to Shelton C. Sherman caught his attention. Never before had Spooky seen the full name written down on paper. He studied it curiously.

"Shelton She Sherman," he read aloud, as he stood the letter up on a shelf. "That's a funny name, *Shel*ton She *Sher*man! C! C, gal ding it! Shelton She—C. Sherman. Say, that's a hell of a name for a man to pack around for folks to stub their tongue on." He fingered another letter and stood it alongside the first. "Shelton She Sherman," he read again.

"You're boozed up, Spooky," Spider accused, coming up behind and resting an arm heavily on Spooky's shoulder. "I'll gamble you had two bottles when you left town—you swine. Why, anybody can read that right off. Anybody that ain't drunk," he amended.

"Le's see you try it," Spooky challenged. "Bet yuh four bits you can't say it straight." He stood a third letter up, and after that a fourth.

"Now read 'em all—just the names—one after another, 'n see who's drunk!" he urged. "Bet yuh four bits yuh can't do it."

Whereupon Spider walked up in front of the shelf, planted his knuckles on his hips and began to read: "Shelton—C—Sherman. Shelton She—C—Sherman. Shelton She Sher—oh, thunder!" he surrendered, shaking his head ruefully. "C'mon, Jim. You try it."

So Jim, showing two-thirds of his teeth in a wide grin, came up and stood beside the two, studied the letter for a moment and fell over the very first C.

"Bet a dollar Shep can't say it himself," he said, and pried off a big chew of tobacco. "Nobody could—sober. If Spooky hadn't went and swallered that hull bottle, I could do it."

"What all yuh talkin' about?" A little old man with bent shoulders and a long, graying mustache came trotting up from

31

a far corner where he had been reading the last *Boise States-man* by a smoky lamp. "When it comes to readin', they ain't a one of yuh that amounts to anything. Yuh can't hardly read a look-out-for-the-cyars sign on a railroad crossin'!" He gummed a wad of tobacco and slid his spectacles farther down toward the end of his high, pointed nose. "What is it you want read out to yuh?"

"Read the names on them four letters, Pike—and read 'em fast," Spider invited, with a wicked little twinkle in his eye. "We got a bet on, who c'n read 'em the fastest."

"Huh! Can't yuh read plain handwritin', none of yuh?" He adjusted his spectacles again. "Shelton She Sherman—"

Spider gave a howl and swung Pike back into his corner. "Shelton She Sherman shells she shells by the sheshore," he stated gravely. "I'll bet a dollar there ain't a man in camp can git that straight."

They all tried it. They were hilariously chanting in chorus that Shelton She Sherman shold she shells when Shelton himself walked in among them, smiling his disarming smile of guileless good nature.

"Why, hello, Shelton She Sherman, who shall shell she shells on the sheshore," Spider greeted him joyously. "Come right in, my boy. You're wanted."

"That's good. I'd hate awfully to think I wasn't wanted," Shelton replied. "Supper over, fellows? I'm hungry as a she bear."

"Shelton She Sherman, the she bear shays she shall not shell she shells—" yelled Spooky, rolling over onto a bed and kicking his heels into the air, and laughing so that he could not go on.

"Say, what's the matter with you fellows, anyway?" Shelton demanded. "Can't you take something for it? Say, Spooky, get any mail for your little friend?"

"Make Shep say it, or don't give 'im his letters," Breed Jim suggested, spitting tobacco juice into the wood box so that he could grin.

"Say what?"

Spider went over and stood guard before the shelf. His face was sober, except for the lurking devil of fun in his eyes. "Here's four letters from mamma and Susie and Sister Ann and the little fairy that works in the candy store on the corner," he informed Shelton. "If you can say, Shelton She Sherman shells she shells by the sheshore—say it right, I mean—you can have 'em."

"No, he can't either!" Spooky interjected, rising up, recovered from his fit. "He can't have but one for every time he says it."

"Hell, he can't have but one try for every letter," put in Jim, coming up.

Shelton took a minute to grasp just what was expected of him. He made Jim repeat the sentence and he said it over under his breath for practise while Jim muddled the words. He peered at the envelopes over Spider's shoulder and his heart swelled with desire.

"Shelton C. Sherman sells sea shells by the sheshore," he recited nonchalantly and reached out his hand for the first letter.

" 'Sheshore'—you can't have it! You done lost that one," chortled Spider. "Try the second one, Shep."

"Oh, say, fellows! That one's from the only mother I've got," pleaded Shelton; but the three were obdurate. The second one he lost, and the third. The fourth, which he suspected of being a bill from his dentist, he refused to try for and went off to get something to eat in the cabin, more than half angry. This was his first mail from home and he had been fighting homesickness from the day he arrived. Shelton C. Sherman loved a joke as well as any one, but he considered this performance just plain cussedness.

- However, he practised faithfully upon the sentence while he ate cold boiled beef, sour-dough bread and a dish of fried corn, and emptied the teapot of reddish, tannin-charged tea. Burney sat smoking before the fire, absorbed in his own thoughts.

So, full fed and feeling more equal to the situation, he hurried back to the bunkhouse.

"Shelton C. Sherman sells sea shells by the seashore," he recited triumphantly, the moment he was inside the door, and grabbed the letter he knew was from his mother. "Aw, I guess you fellows are not so smart," he taunted.

"Shelton C. Sherman sells sea shells by the seashore—and

33

takes number two—and that from my best girl, fellows. Shelton C. Sherman continues to sell sea shells by the seashore, and gathers in his tender missive from his big sister. And Shelton C. Sherman doesn't care a hang whether he shall sell sea shells by the seashore at your service, because that other letter bears all the earmarks of being a gentle reminder of a very painful hour spent in the torture chamber of one Painless Perkins, who purports to pull cuspids, bicuspids or molars without pain to himself or money refunded. Thanks awfully, my dear friends. Anything else before I seat myself to peruse these loving messages from home?"

"No fair greasin' your tongue, Shep," Spooky complained. "You ought to be spanked for stayin' out so late, anyway. Where yuh been?"

"Hunting spooks. Shooting rattlesnakes. Talking to a pretty girl. Don't bother me, fellers."

While Spider fidgeted, Shelton seated himself in a chair by the lamp, tilted the chair back comfortably against the wall, and through the medium of his letters mentally projected himself into the midst of his family circle back home.

CHAPTER SEVEN

"STAY AWAY FROM PIUTE HILLS"

SPIDER was in the mood to tease some one, and Shelton seemed the logical victim.

"Shootin' rattlesnakes, yuh say?" he inquired banteringly, by way of starting an argument. He elicited a grunt of assent from Shelton and no further notice.

"I used to shoot snakes some myself," Spider observed reminiscently. "It's easy. Yuh see a snake—just like it was over there, say—and you full your old gat and cut down on 'im like this, say—and *bing!*" While he spoke, he matched the words with action, drawing his gun and firing a bullet between the feet of Shelton C. Sherman, splintering the chair round.

"Oh, say! Cut it out, can't you? I'm reading," Shelton reproved mildly, without looking up from the letter.

"And when you see another one—*bang!*" This time Spider

made a slight miscalculation and nicked the leather of Shelton's bootheel.

"Say! Look where you're shooting, why don't you? How do you expect a fellow to read—"

"By golly, there's another one!" Spider shot again, this time being careful to aim at the floor beneath Shelton's chair.

"And there's one, right by your ear!" Roused to action, Shelton whipped out his own revolver and sent a bullet humming past Spider's head. "Look out! There's one right behind you!"

Spider gave a squawk and rolled off his chair in his haste to put himself out of range. "Aw, I was only joshing, Shep!" he cried reproachfully. "You don't want to take things so damn serious. I never meant nothin'."

"Neither did I," Shelton retorted. "What shall we do now? Go on playing snakes?"

"No, by golly!" To prove it, Spider broke his gun, emptied the remaining cartridges into his palm and threw the six-shooter on his bed.

"What're you fellows grinning your heads off about?" he demanded fretfully of Spooky and Jim. "How'd I know the kid could hit where he aimed at? Stands a feller in hand to duck and duck quick, by thunder, when a strange hand points a gun at yuh."

"I didn't duck, did I?" Shelton cut in shrewdly. "And I didn't know how straight you could shoot, either. I took a chance, same as a fellow has to take if he wants to have any pleasure in life. Same as the girl said I took when I went down into the snakes' den to get the rattles off the dead ones."

"Yes, you did—not!"

"Yes, I did too!" and Shelton produced several rattles with the pinched-off place still showing fresh. "And that's only half. I divided with the girl, just to show what a nice, generous boy I can be. Besides, she shot a lot of 'em herself."

"What gyurl was that?" Roused again from his reading by the disturbance, Pike peered at Shelton over his spectacles.

"Oh, a girl named Vida. She lives in a sheep wagon over somewhere near the Haunted Hills. I don't know her last name. She keeps house for Poppy and Uncle Jake."

Pike laid down his paper, took the spectacles from his nose, folded down the bows and produced a long, metal case while he gummed his wad of tobacco thoughtfully.

"Which side of the Haunted Hills is her folks ranging sheep on?" he asked, in the tone of a prosecuting attorney examining a witness for the defense. Pike had that portentous manner when he approached anything pertaining to the welfare of the Sunbeam.

"Why, I don't know. Somewhere around close, I should judge, because it was after five when she said she must go and get supper for Poppy." Shelton glanced hungrily at his letters, though he was too polite to say that he would like very much to be left in peace while he read them.

Pike was making ready for another truth-compelling question when Burney opened the door and came stooping in, his little eyes boring through the haze of powder smoke that still hung heavy in the low-ceilinged room.

Spider, Spooky and Jim looked at one another apprehensively. The other two met Burney's sharp glances unmoved; Pike because he could think of only one thing at a time and his mind happened to be preoccupied with the presence of sheep in the country, and Shelton because the emotion called fear had yet to be born within him. During the complete silence that fell upon the group, Shelton tore open another letter and unfolded the pages, which crackled sharply.

"What's all this shootin' about?" Burney's voice might be high and thin and wholly lacking in the timbre one would expect from a man of his size, but the sentence cut deep.

"Oh—nothin'. I was just foolin' with my gun—just—kinda seein' how she worked." Spider fumbled with his book of cigarette papers, awkwardly trying to single out a leaf.

Pike, still ruminating upon the one idea that filled his mind for the moment, unconsciously relieved the situation.

"Say, Burney, them Williams sheep must be a crowdin' up on our range," he announced suddenly. "The boy hyar says he seen a gyurl that belongs to a sheep outfit foolin' around Spook Hills. I know old Sam Williams has got a gyurl, but I never knowed she ever come out and camped with 'im. Still, she's liable to uh done it, if Shep here's tellin' the truth."

"She's done it irrespective of my telling the truth," Shelton observed and went on with his letter.

Burney stood stooped forward, like a menacing presence hovering over the men, and stared hard at Pike and Shelton, and at the three others who avoided meeting his sharp little eyes. He reached out a great paw and fumbled for the door latch.

"You want to cut out this shooting around here," he said to Spider, in the tone of the master speaking to his man. "Guns ain't made to play with."

He pulled open the door and stood hesitating on the threshold, his great head and shoulders still thrust within the room. "Come on out here, kid; I want to see yuh," he commanded and withdrew into the night.

Shelton sighed and folded up his letter. It seemed to him, then, that the one thing he missed most at the Sunbeam was neither companionship nor the creature comforts of life, but privacy. Waking or sleeping, he was never quite sure of being left undisturbed for five minutes together, and that in a land where isolation is the keynote of life.

He went out, wondering what Burney could possibly want him to do at this time of night, or what he could want to see him about that could not be spoken of before the others. So far as he had observed the men of the Sunbeam, not one of the lot—unless it should be Burney himself—ever had a thought he would not share; nor anything else, for that matter, except his saddle horse and riding gear.

Burney was waiting for him outside and without a word he led the way over to the cabin where he lived and where the men all ate together. He went inside, stooping to pass through the doorway, and Shelton followed him. He hoped that whatever business it was that Burney had with him, it would not take many minutes.

Burney went to his plank stool and sat down, leaning over the smoldering coals in the rough fireplace. His great hands were clasped together and his forearms rested upon his huge knees.

"Whereabouts did you go to-day when you met that girl?" he asked abruptly, transfixing the young man with a sharp glance.

"Well, I don't know that I could tell, exactly." Shelton's honest blue eyes returned Burney's look unafraid. "I just

37

headed out toward the hills and let Dutch pick his own trail. He was climbing most of the time."

"How long did you set there talking to that girl?"

"Well, I don't know that, either. You must remember, Mr. Burney. I was just out fooling around and didn't pay any attention to distance or the time I spent." With his underlip caught between his teeth, he considered the matter dutifully. "I suppose I must have been there on the ledge two or three hours altogether," he said. "I remember that the shadows were about as long as they would be in the middle of the afternoon, and it must have been five o'clock or later when she finally said she had to go home."

Burney stared into the fire. "Which way did she go when she left yuh?"

"Why, straight on beyond where I had gone. That is, she kept on going and I rode back this way."

"Did yuh come back the same way you went?"

"Yes, I'm pretty sure that I did."

Burney studied the coals as if he were looking for something among the embers. "See—anybody?" He asked the question gruffly. Almost as if he were ashamed to be asking it.

Shelton laughed, a little chuckle of chagrin.

"I tried to see somebody," he said, in an odd tone of diffidence. "I thought I heard some one coming behind me and I'm pretty sure Dutch heard something too. But whenever I would stop and look around, there wasn't a thing I could see or hear. Then, as soon as I started on again, I'd hear it."

"What? Any idea what it sounded like?"

"Oh—just footsteps of some sort. I've read about cougars and mountain lions and panthers following people in the dark —but they wouldn't make any noise walking, would they?"

Burney turned his eyes toward Shelton for a quick glance. Shelton laughed again.

"Of course, it's all nonsense, but I thought maybe it was that spook the boys talk about."

"There ain't no such thing," Burney said harshly. "But yuh want to keep away from Piute Hills," he added peevishly. "They's—snakes and things. A man's liable to get bit."

Surprised, Shelton looked at him. It was a mighty poor reason to give a man, he could not help thinking. He grinned.

"Well, there aren't as many snakes as there was this morning," he retorted. "The girl and I together killed about sixteen. Here are half the rattles I collected. I gave her the other half."

Burney never glanced toward Shelton's outstretched palm. "You better keep away from them hills. It ain't no place for yuh over there," he repeated vaguely.

"Well—" Shelton was going to argue the point. But Burney turned his back and bent farther over the coals, by his very posture giving Shelton to understand that the subject was closed.

So Shelton went quietly out and returned to the bunkhouse and his letters, considerably puzzled and with a formless dread in the back of his mind. But he dismissed the whole thing from his thoughts and read his letters in what one might call peace, since the rambunctious ones were wrangling amicably over a game of solo, and Pike had gone to bed.

CHAPTER EIGHT

SO HE GOES AT ONCE

N ATURALLY, since Shelton had been warned to stay away from the Haunted Hills, he determined to go again as soon as possible. Burney might have known that, if he had stopped to consider the matter at all; he must surely have known something of human nature, and that he put the spurs to Shelton's curiosity merely proved how deeply absorbed he was in his own affairs.

There was another reason why Shelton wanted to go and that was the girl. She was pretty, no getting around that. And she had a way with her which kept him dwelling upon the things she had said, the way she had looked when she said them and the tones of her voice.

So Shelton rode back to the Haunted Hills, and while he was yet afar off from the ledge on the gully's rim he saw the girl riding slowly down the brushy ridge. He reined in that direction and urged old Dutch into a stiff-legged lope. He looked very pleased and satisfied with himself, plainly expecting a glowing welcome.

Shakespeare once declared that welcome ever smiles. He was wrong; there was no appreciable smile in the welcome Shelton received. Shelton's grin drew itself in at the corners when he came close enough to see the blank composure of her face.

"Hello, Shep," she greeted him uninterestedly, when he was almost alongside. "Why this mad haste? The scenery isn't going to run anywhere and hide, nor the snakes either." And she added as an afterthought, "Neither am I."

Shelton wrinkled his eyebrows. "Are you wishing the scenery would run away and hide?" he asked, consciously adopting the light and frivolous tone he had always employed toward a pretty girl giving an exhibition of temperament.

"I don't care what it does. I only wish I could go somewhere and hide." Her face settled into a brooding discontent with life, such as sometimes seizes the lonely.

"Well, the hiding looks pretty good around here," Shelton suggested amiably. "By the way, how is our rabbit?"

"All right, I guess," she said indifferently. "The darn thing died. I told you it would. I packed it all the way home and got all over fleas, and it went to work and died before supper was ready. I gave it to the dogs."

Again Shelton wrinkled his eyebrows, wishing that she were different. Judging from her attitude toward the rabbit, she had no fine sentiments whatever. Any other girl would have cherished it. Maybe even cried a little when it died. She would not have thrown it out to the dogs.

"That great, overgrown Goliath of yours thinks he's going to play hob, doesn't he?" she demanded abruptly, looking with resentment at Shelton.

Here, he felt, lay the key to her ill humor. He braced himself mentally to meet her latent antagonism.

"Why? How has he managed to win your disfavor? He's been staying right at the ranch all the time—"

"That's all you know about it. He came over to our camp yesterday and told Poppy we were on his range and he'd thank us to get off it. You'd think he owns the whole of Idaho! I was in the wagon washing dishes and I heard him. We'd just had our breakfast. And he acted like he owned us, body and soul.

40

"I stuck my head out of the wagon and asked him where he got his license to come bossing us around, and why didn't he let his own business keep him busy, and he wilted right down! But he certainly talked awful to Poppy—Uncle Jake was out with his sheep and didn't hear him, or there would have been something doing right then and there."

"Why, I don't see why he should want to make you any trouble. There must be some misunderstanding," Shelton said placatingly. "I'm sure there's plenty of range for every one. We drove over miles and miles of it when I was coming to the ranch, and Spooky said it was all Sunbeam range."

"Well, he told Poppy to move right away from Piute Hills, and keep away. And we're not going to. There's better water and better grass, what there is of it, in these hills than anywhere around. He wanted us to go back toward Pillar Butte with our sheep—but he'll find out he's not running the Williams outfit, yet."

Shelton began to look uneasy, as if he were being held responsible in some way for Burney's arrogance. "Well, I certainly knew nothing about it," he said earnestly. "If I had, I probably would have gotten in bad myself by trying to show him where he's wrong. I'm sure there's some mistake. Perhaps he felt that you were encroaching—"

"He felt that he wanted to hog the range," Vida interrupted him hotly. "But he isn't going to get away with it; not with us, anyway. We have just as much right here as he has, and we're not afraid of him just because he's as big as all outdoors."

"He certainly is big, and yet he's kind of gentle too. I simply can't see him playing the part of oppressor, somehow."

"You're just letting him pull the wool over your eyes. He looks mean and he *is* mean. But *I'm* not afraid of him—I'd stand up to forty more just as big as he is, if it would help Poppy."

Shelton laughed. "Well, Vida is the feminine of David, didn't you say? David and Goliath—oh, say, that's rich! I must write that home to the folks. A girl David, at that. Where's your slingshot?"

"You shut up! I'm not in the mood to joke about him. It's

all right for you. You can stand back and see how funny it is, and write about it to your folks. But it isn't funny to *us,* Mr. Pretty Boy. It means our living, and being able to finish school, and paying for the home we've got mortgaged in Boise, if you want to know."

"Well, of course I didn't mean—"

She stopped him with a gesture. "Do you suppose I don't like pretty clothes?" Her eyes blazed at him from under her old felt hat which her father had cast aside. "Do you think I *like* to live like a squaw, and tie my hair up with a grocery string, and wear these—" She gave an unexpected little sob, wholly feminine and disturbing.

"I'm living this way so Poppy can get ahead of the game enough to afford something better for himself. I couldn't bear to stay in school and think of him living out here in a smelly old sheep wagon. I thought I could help him hurry up and make money enough so that he could sell out, or put the sheep out on shares, or something, and live in town with me. I *hate* it! I hate the sight of sheep. But sheep are the only thing Poppy sees good money in, and this is about the only place that isn't overstocked already. And that great, big, whiny-voiced bully can just leave us alone! We're not hurting him any."

"I'm sure you're not," Shelton said soothingly. "I certainly will do all I can—"

"Poppy sold out to him two years ago, just to keep from having trouble with him, and tried to go into something else. And he lost about half his money and just had to get back into sheep, because they're the only thing he's sure of making good at. That's why he went broke before—because when Mother died he wanted to start some business in town, so I wouldn't have to live like this. He had to mortgage the place to get into sheep again. And he isn't going to sell out now to please anybody. He's going to run his sheep in these hills just as long as he wants to, and you Sunbeamers have just got to stand for it. If you don't like it, why, you can lump it."

"I *do* like it," Shelton declared hastily. "You mustn't say or think that we're all against you and wanting you to leave here, because that isn't true. I'm not against you and I want you to stay around here just as long as I stay."

42

But Vida refused to be cheered by that statement. "You're mighty small potatoes when it comes to this range business," she reminded him. "And when I say *you* have got to stand for our running sheep here, I mean the outfit you're stopping with; you Sunbeamers. We're going to stay. We've got to, or get out of the sheep business, and Poppy isn't going to do that until he's out of debt. There's going to be good money in sheep this year," she added, with pitiful optimism. "Wool is up and the lamb crop was fine."

So she talked and Shelton presently attempted to change the subject. To him, it seemed a waste of time for a girl as pretty as Vida to sit there talking about sheep and range feuds and the like. She shouldn't be obliged to think of those things. She should, he thought privately, think a little about him.

Anyway, it looked like a big enough country for all the people there were in it. Big enough for thousands and thousands of sheep, and cattle too. And farther up in the Haunted Hills he could see that there was timber worthy the name.

There was so much of it! For one lone cattleman and one lone sheep owner to quarrel over this big feeding ground looked childishly unnecessary. Shelton tried hard enough but he could not get the girl's point of view. He could not believe that Burney was the range hog she seemed to believe him. It seemed to him that she was rather inclined to make a mountain out of a mole-hill.

CHAPTER NINE

SHELTON HUNTS SPOOKS

That day they did not shoot snakes. Instead, they rode to the brink of a deep, fearsome-looking cañon where Vida stopped. She stared long all up and down it, looking for caves, she said. She did not seem to care enough about them, however, to go down and explore the rocky walls. Her mood was still enmeshed in the net of circumstances and environment, and her thoughts ran upon the everyday sordidness of her life.

She told Shelton how she had sent to Pocatello by one of

43

their herders for a pair of shoes and that they didn't fit. She wondered how she was going to manage an exchange—there being no prospect of her getting to town herself for goodness knows when. Shelton offered to go for her but she would not hear to that.

He tried to talk of his home and the things he had seen and done, but Vida kept harking back to the petty details of her own life. The other day she had listened hungrily to his talk of the towns. He could not understand why she should seem so different, so circumscribed in her interests, to-day. Shelton, you see, had never confronted any of the big problems of life—particularly the big economic problems.

They turned up the cañon, skirting it to the very foot of one of the steeper hills. Shelton was beginning to think of starting home from very boredom—except that the Sunbeam ranch, with its sun-baked area of sand and its little, squalid cabins and no human being on the place, unless Burney were home, spelled a boredom more complete than this.

"This hill's full of caves," Vida informed him apathetically, pointing a grimy hand to a rugged slope. "I was around here seven or eight years ago. Poppy used to be a prospector and he prospected all through these hills.

"It was a claim he sold that put him in the sheep business in the first place. One summer I came with him—the summer after Mother died. I could show you all kinds of caves and places, around here."

"Well, why don't you? Maybe we could land that spook the boys claim is in these hills. Come on—let's do some exploring!"

"I don't feel like it; and we'd need candles, anyway. Some day we might bring some and I'll take you through the biggest ones—if I can find them again. I'll have to go back pretty quick; I'm baking bread to-day and it rises awfully fast these hot days."

"Oh, say! Do come on and help me hunt spooks," Shelton pleaded, suddenly realizing how much he hated to have her ride off and leave him. "Honest, there is a ghost. Spooky saw it, and Spider, and so did Jim. It follows folks at dusk—though maybe we could rout it out in daytime if we try real hard—and if you turn back and try to run it down, it

44

gives a horrible screech and disappears into the bowels of the earth. Come on. Let's you and me go spook hunting!" In his eagerness to persuade her, his tone was much more ardent than he had intended.

Vida settled her disreputable old hat more firmly on her head because of the wind that had risen and looked at him unmoved.

"What makes you act so silly?" she inquired impatiently. "You smiled at me then just the way one of our herders does when he gets about half-shot. He always thinks he's in love with me then, and hangs around the wagon trying to propose, until Poppy has to chase him off. Last time, I set old Whimper on him." She turned away from Shelton's flush of embarrassment and began to study the bold wall of rocks opposite them. "There are lions in these hills—panthers, maybe you'd call them—and now and then a black bear; and all kinds of lynx and bobcats and coyotes and things. But there aren't any spooks. I guess it wouldn't take more than a bobcat to put you Sunbeamers on the run, though. I suppose maybe they saw a coyote and imagined it was a ghost."

"After that unkind thrust," sighed Shelton, with exaggerated reproach meant to cover his resentment at her disdain of a moment ago, "I shall have to leave thee. Farewell, heartless one, until we meet under more auspicious skies." And he added, with some malice, "Let your half-drunken sheep herder try that."

"There isn't anything the matter with this sky," said Vida, "and my half-drunken sheep herder quotes Shakespeare, if you please. Last time some one brought a bottle into camp, he spouted about a third of 'Midsummer Night's Dream'; all the mushy parts. That's why I set the dog on him. I wish to goodness you would go, if you're going to act like that." The worst of it was, she meant exactly what she said; looking into her eyes, he could not doubt it.

Shelton considered himself very much offended. He turned away with a crisp good-by and rode back down along the cañon wall. He did not look back, though he would have given a good deal to have seen her face when he left her.

"I'll be up here somewhere day after tomorrow," she called after him, when he had ridden fifty yards or so.

45

"I won't," he called back and rode on. After a while he began to wonder if she had heard him. At first he wished that he had spoken louder; later on, he was sorry that he had spoken so loudly.

He found a place where the cañon looked crossable and rode down into it. Then he discovered that the opposite side, which from the farther rim had seemed to have a crude trail zigzagging up to the top, was buttressed at the bottom with a ledge so steep that even he knew better than ask Dutch to climb it.

The way down the cañon was blocked by what must have been a waterfall at one time in the past, but was now a sheer jump-off of ten feet or more. He did not ask Dutch to go down that, either. Of necessity, then, he went up the cañon towards the hills—reluctantly, because Vida might see him from the top and suspect him of hanging around in her vicinity because he was like that sheep herder who got drunk and spouted Shakespeare all over the place.

As he rode along, the cañon widened until there was a grassy bottom with a little creek that kept the place green. Then it narrowed abruptly, with black ledges leaning forward. It became so gloomy and dark down there at last that Shelton looked at his watch to see if it were not nearly night.

He was not riding, now, but plodding along afoot, with old Dutch following patiently along behind him; and the way in which Dutch negotiated the scattered rocks and deep little washouts proved him the best of his kind.

The cañon walls drew in to hold close in its clasp a huge thicket of chokecherries, serviceberry bushes and buckbush, mingled together in one glorious tangle. The ground was soft and black and rich-looking where he skirted the thicket, and somewhere near him he heard water gurgling like a newly awakened baby talking to its fists. The sound merely reminded him, however, that he was thirsty.

Leaving Dutch standing with dropped reins, he went forward, parting the branches before him with both hands to make easy passing. In a minute or two he came to a tiny stream, evidently fed by some hidden spring and bordered with mint and dainty little grass flowers growing in the deep shade of the thicket.

He felt all the thrill of discovery. He was sure that Vida did not know of this cold little brook, else she surely would have spoken of it. She had looked into the cañon and had not mentioned that there was water down there. Probably no white man had ever drunk from it before, he thought exultantly, as he knelt down on the vivid green margin so sharply contrasting with the black barrenness all around.

He leaned far over to drink and then suddenly drew back, staring fixedly at something in the soft, black soil at the very edge. A huge imprint in the ooze; a track so fresh that even Shelton, new to the ways of the wild though he was, could not fail to see that it was but minutes old—seconds, perhaps.

He sat back on his heels and looked at it, puzzling over what manner of beast would have made it. Huge, almost human, it looked—big as the great tracks Burney made when he walked in the sand—and yet not human. From all angles Shelton studied it. Like the print of a great, bare foot it was, except that the toes were not the toe prints of a man; nor was the track shaped just like a man's foot.

Shelton pulled off his own boot and sock, stamped his foot into the mud alongside the other track and studied the two imprints curiously. Even while he stared at them, the water pushed the mud back in, smoothing out little details and making of the big track a long, formless depression in the ooze. Looking at it then, Shelton saw how much it resembled his own, except in size. Had he seen it thus at first, he would have called it a man's track and let it go at that. But it was not a man's track, he was positive of that. Seen when the two were fresh, it in no way resembled his own.

"Must have been a bear," he told himself at last, while he washed his foot and put on his sock and boot. "She said there were bears in the hills—but say, he certainly must be a whopper, to make a track the size of that one! Too bad the beggar got off without my seeing it."

He knelt and got his drink from the brook, then stood up and pulled out his gun and examined it. Pretty small caliber to go hunting the bear that made that track, but Shelton did want to kill a bear, now that he knew there was one about. Maybe the fellows back at the ranch would let up on their infernal joshing if he brought one into camp. They couldn't patronize him any longer and treat him as if he were about ten years old. And if he could send a bearskin rug home to his mother—one that he had killed himself—say! That would be simply great!

Foolhardily he searched beyond the brook, though the tangle was thick and much too favorable to an ambush. He was not scared. But he was terribly thrilled and excited. He beat about in the bushes with a noise that would have sent even a bear careening out of the cañon, and then came crashing out into the open near the northern wall of the cañon. There he stood baffled and disappointed before the emptiness.

Surely the creature could not have climbed that sheer wall; and yet Shelton had a hazy notion that bears did climb trees and things. He was staring up at it and wondering what possible route the beast could have taken—since it did not seem to be anywhere in the cañon—when he noticed the gorgeous purple and crimson of the sky. Sunset so soon? It is astonishing how the hours slide past when one is wholly given up to that primitive emotion, the lust of the chase.

He must start back to the ranch, though he hated the idea of leaving that bear alive. He went back to where Dutch was waiting impatiently, with twitching ears and uneasy tramplings, mounted and started back down the cañon. In the narrowest places the gloom of night was already filling the gorge almost to the brim, and Dutch stepped out briskly, wherever the footing was passable.

Then a strange sensation seized Shelton C. Sherman. He looked back without quite knowing why he did so. The cañon yawned stark and empty behind. He shrugged his shoulders and rode on. Presently he turned again and looked. vaguely expectant. There was nothing. Then it came definitely,—the conviction that he was being followed.

He stopped Dutch still and waited, watching the gorge behind him; listening, too, for a betraying rattle among the rocks or even a faint rustling among the bushes. There was no sign of any living thing save himself and Dutch, and a belated bird that flew chirping up to the higher slopes. Dutch thrust out his nose, pulling for slack in the reins, which was his way of saying that he wanted to go. The hide along his neck and shoulders twitched and quivered, which was another sign that Dutch was not at all easy in his mind.

Shelton was not frightened, as the word is commonly understood. He was puzzled, however, and he felt an eerie prickling of the flesh as the darkness advanced. But mainly he was half angry because he could not see to shoot—even supposing there was something to shoot at.

Once after that he heard a rock rattle down and bump somewhere—and the sound was so close behind him that he pulled his six-shooter from its holster and turned for a shot at the bear, or whatever it was. But Dutch was pulling harder on the reins and stepping along much faster than was wise, and would not wait until the thing overtook them.

It was Dutch that found the trail up the cañon side where they had come down some hours before. Shelton could feel the quivering of the horse's flesh beneath his legs, and it dawned upon him that old Dutch was scared and was climbing the hill faster than he ought to climb. He supposed that he really ought to get off and walk. He dismounted then and went on ahead.

He wondered if he really felt more comfortable in his mind when Dutch walked between him and the bear. To test his own feeling about the matter, he looped the reins awkwardly around the saddle horn and let Dutch take the lead for a few rods. But he found himself constantly looking behind him, and he soon decided that he was really more comfortable walking ahead and leading Dutch.

At the top he tried to persuade himself that his imagination was playing him tricks; that there was nothing behind him save the bleak, dark hills and the usual night prowlers abroad on business that concerned only themselves. But there was Dutch, hurrying along with his eyes rolled to watch the trail behind. He could not credit Dutch with having too much imagination.

Before he had gone a quarter of a mile farther, Shelton was clinging to the saddle horn while the horse galloped unevenly over the rough ground. It takes a rider with some experience to sit easily in the saddle and ride headlong through the sagebrush country, with a jump here, a quick swerve there, and a longer stride to bridge a cut or avoid one of those bugbears of the range, gopher and badger holes.

Shelton had all these things to contend with and he had also the natural roughness of Dutch's gait. Ordinarily the mere feat of riding at a fast gallop was quite sufficient to occupy all of his attention. To-night, however, the weird feeling that he was still being followed persisted in his mind.

Before he reached the brow of the hill, beneath which winked the welcome lights of the Sunbeam cabins, Shelton C. Sherman came as near to being scared as he had ever been in his twenty-one years of heedless existence.

He was riding with his head turned over his shoulder and his eyes strained into the darkness behind him, when from the rear there came the most horrible screech he had ever heard or imagined. His hair rose on his scalp. Dutch gave a leap ahead that almost unseated him and ran like a scared jackrabbit down the hill and into the Sunbeam yard.

CHAPTER TEN

THE KILLING BEGINS

Say, fellows, how big is a bear that makes a track so long?" Shelton measured a space with his spread palms and waited for some one to volunteer the information.

"About as big as a good-sized elephant," drawled Spider, after a perceptible pause, while he held a lighted match to his cigarette.

"No, but *really?* You know, I ran across a fresh bear track that was that long. I couldn't find the bear, though. I hunted all around without getting a glimpse of it. It seems strange that I didn't, because the track was perfectly fresh—just made, in fact—"

"How d' yuh know it was?" Spooky demanded, looking up from the quirt he was mending.

"Well, it was right at the edge of a little stream of water, and the water hadn't washed any mud into it yet when I first saw it. And at the heel, the grass was just beginning to stand up straight again after being mashed down. I thought that must mean the track was fresh."

"Purty good, for a pilgrim," Breed Jim observed dryly, shifting his cud of tobacco to the other cheek and grinning.

Shelton eyed him doubtfully for a moment. "I suppose you think I'm just imagining the whole thing," he said defensively. "I'm sure it was a bear track, though. I've always read they look very much like a man's track, and this one did—until I took off my boot and made a track of my own alongside it. I could tell then that there was a lot of difference."

"You *what?* With that track as fresh as you claim?" Spider's face showed blank incredulity.

"Why, yes. I had to make sure, didn't I? It certainly was a big track. It was at least twice as long as mine and three or four times as wide, I should think. I didn't take time to measure exactly; I wish now I had. I'd have some actual figures to show you fellows."

"Shelton She Sherman says she shaw a she bear shelling sea shells on the sheshore," Spider commented gravely, with the well-known twinkle in his eyes.

"Aw, say, fellows!" Shelton protested, for the thing was all too vivid in his memory. "It's a fact, all of it." He went over the story, giving every detail which he could remember.

Spider got up, threw his cigarette stub into the fire and turned upon Spooky.

"Say, Spooky, you're to blame for this," he sternly accused. "Shep was a nice, innocent, truthful cuss when he come here. But you've lied to him, and you've lied before him, and you've lied behind his back ever since he hit the ranch. We can't blame him for thinkin' that's the proper way to act. He is more to be pitied than censured.

"If Shelton She Sherman says he shes she bears shelling sea shells on the sheshore, why, it's your fault and his misfortune. If possible, we must keep this from his folks back home. And if there's anything we can do to remedy the evil before it becomes virelent and the whole damn outfit gets infecticated, I for one am ready to do my part. But if this turns out fatal, it's you that'll have to bear the blame."

Shelton laughed. So did Spooky, for that matter, and Jim and Pike. Afterwards, Shelton protested so earnestly that he was telling the truth that they consented at last to believe he had seen a track which may have looked to him like a bear's track, and also the possibility that he had been followed by something.

"But that wasn't any bear," Spooky insisted with perfect sincerity. "It was that same spook I felt and seen and I'll bet money on it. Fu'thermore, bears don't screech the way you say that thing done. You want to keep away from them hills, Shep. I've got a hunch that thing is fixin' to git somebuddy. Here's four of us been follered, now. There ain't a one of us that wouldn't swear to it. Lemme tell yuh, Shep, them hills ain't safe for nobody."

There was more talk along that line; two hours and more of it, as a matter of fact. And the result was that the very next morning Shelton C. Sherman borrowed Spider's big forty-five six-shooter and cartridge belt and stuffed it with cartridges; borrowed Spooky's skinning knife and fastened that in the belt; put up lunch enough to last him two meals, dodged Burney and Burney's coldly questioning eyes, and rode back to the Haunted Hills to hunt for the bear that made so enormous a track that none of the boys would believe him when he told how big it was. Spider had assured him that his six gun would sure make it unhealthy for any bear in the country, providing Shep wasn't too scared to shoot straight. Shelton also had his own thirty-eight, and he had some skill in shooting—witness the rattles he took home with him after that first expedition.

No one worried much about Shelton's personal welfare. They were not the worrying kind, for one thing, and they trusted a good deal to Dutch. So they fitted him out and let him go hunt his bear, and they helped him to avoid Burney, who most certainly would have forbidden him to go.

First, Shelton rode straight to where he might hope to meet Vida. He meant to lend her his own revolver, if she should desire to come along. He was so eager for the meeting that he should have suspected his real feeling toward her. But he did not. He came upon her just as he was topping the high ridge that would give him a wide outlook in the direction of her camp. She urged her horse forward and her eyes were hard and angry when she came close to him.

"Say, you Sunbeamers are certainly going to a lot of trouble to be neighborly, aren't you?" she demanded, without replying to his gay greeting. "I don't mean you, personally," she added more gently. "But I'm so stirred up this morning

I'd just like to go over and fight the whole outfit. Do you know what Goliath has done now?"

"Why, nothing at all except stay at the ranch and act like a hippopotamus with a toothache," Shelton answered mildly.

"That isn't all he's done," she retorted sharply. "What was he doing last night, do you suppose?"

"Why, nothing, so far as I know. He was at home when I got there—and I was late getting in. He was sitting in front of the fire smoking, the way he always is at night, until he goes to bed."

"That's all you know about it. He was over to our camp, killing off about two dozen of our sheep; that's where he was. It couldn't have been any one else but Goliath. He twisted their necks like you'd wring the neck of a chicken!"

"Twisted their—necks?"

"That's what I said. Uncle Jake was with that bunch down in the foothills behind the butte. He heard the dogs and went out, but it was dark and he couldn't see what was wrong. One of the dogs was killed too," she added grimly. "Neck twisted just like the sheep. And you know very well who did that. No ordinary man could wring a sheep's neck the way theirs were wrung.

"And the dog must have been just grabbed up and *squashed!* I saw him this morning, and his ribs are all smashed and his neck broken. It was Laddie and he wasn't afraid. Uncle Jake says the other dog just crept under the wagon and whined and wouldn't come out."

"Oh, say, doesn't that sound more as if an animal had been around?" Shelton cut in eagerly. "You know, I went down in that cañon over there after I left you and I saw a bear track. A whopper of a track, it was. The boys wouldn't believe me when I told them how big it was. Why, it was that long!" Shelton measured the length again with his spread palms and again he saw frank disbelief in the eyes that watched him. "Honest," he added, when he saw how she doubted his word.

"But Uncle Jake *did* see a little bit, just as he was leaving," Vida argued. "He saw him go over a little rise, running; and he was big—Uncle Jake would swear that it was Goliath. A bear wouldn't run on its hind legs—"

"It might, if it were carrying something. Don't you suppose it would carry a sheep away with it?" He leaned toward her, his cheeks flushed with earnestness. "I'm positive Burney was not away from the ranch last night," he said. "I could almost swear to it."

Vida shook her head but it was plain that her conviction was shaken a bit. She let her eyes waver from his face and she saw then how he was armed. She pointed to the sagging gun belt and the weapon that hung at his hip.

"Is that for the bear?" she asked, with her first smile that day.

"It certainly is, and I brought mine along for you, if you'll take a hand in the hunt. Come on! I'll take you to where I saw his track and then maybe we can find some trail to his den."

Vida threw back her head and laughed musically, with the unrestrained laughter of one used to wide spaces. "Oh, you're the funniest thing alive!" she told him. "Are you planning to have me eaten up? Is it customary to invite a lady to go bear hunting with you at the risk of her life?"

"Oh, I beg your pardon. It never occurred to me that perhaps there might be some risk attached to it," Shelton declared, so convincingly in earnest that she went off into another fit of laughter.

"I wouldn't want you to be hurt, but I'm so horribly green at this bear hunting that perhaps you wouldn't be quite safe with me. I think perhaps I'd better go alone. It certainly must be an enormous bear."

"Aren't you afraid, yourself?" Vida studied his face.

"Afraid? Why, I never thought about that. Do you think a man would have any reason to be afraid of a bear with a track this long?" For the third time he measured the space more or less accurately with his two hands.

"Oh, get along with you and bring me his hide, then!" Vida seemed to have suddenly decided that he was making fun of her. "I'll trail along on high ground, where I can kind of keep an eye on you. They say danger lies half in being afraid of it, anyway, so you should be fairly safe."

An hour or more after that, Shelton dismounted from old Dutch at the little stream that led down from the upper cañon. He thought he had discovered another bear track but he was too ignorant to be sure. In a narrow strip of loose sand which bordered the stream there was the deep imprint of what looked very much like a heel; a bear heel, he thought, though a flat rock just even with the surface of the sand had received the weight of the rest of the foot and left no mark to tell exactly what it was.

For a few minutes Shelton blundered about in that immediate neighborhood, found nothing more and went on. At the place in the thicket where he had found the track, there was nothing now save two faint depressions in the mud. And since that was his only clue to the beast he sought, he was patiently discouraged. He went down to where he had left Dutch and turned to ride back whence he had come; at least, as far as the place where he had seen that mark.

CHAPTER ELEVEN

SHELTON LEARNS ABOUT FEAR

A NARROW GORGE which he had overlooked before, thinking it a mere rift in the piled bowlders, he now decided to investigate. He was in no hurry to ride back to the upland and report failure to Vida, who would laugh at him for a greenhorn. Besides, he had a vague impression that bears were rather fond of rough places.

This was rough enough, in all conscience; even when he pulled upon the reins and clucked encouragingly, Dutch did not want to follow him over some of the worst places. He told himself that the sagacity and sure-footedness of the range horse has been greatly overestimated, but if you should see the places where he coaxed Dutch to risk his poor old bones, you would feel a new sympathy and respect for that sore-tried animal.

Presently the gorge began to widen so that it was possible to ride instead of scrambling afoot over the rocks. And then, just as he was coming into another grassy bottom, he saw before him—faintly defined it is true, but unmistakable—the print of that great foot which still looked weirdly human to his town-trained eyes.

Shelton C. Sherman gave a suppressed whoop and went forward eagerly. So little did he know of the wild that he fully expected to ride joyously with the hide of the biggest bear in all Idaho neatly rolled and tied behind the cantle of his saddle. Later it occurred to him that he should have measured that track, so he might confound Spooky and Spider, chief doubters at the Sunbeam, with actual figures. But he was too far up the cañon before he thought of it and he would not turn back then.

Shelton went on and on—a mile, he guessed it afterward, though in rough country such as that, distance is difficult to estimate correctly. Eventually he came out into a crude amphitheater formed by the converging hills. On one side the ascent was almost sheer, with loose shale that made it impossible to climb, even for a bear. Shelton was sure of that, after he had tried to go up, and after Dutch had planted both feet stiffly before him and refused even to attempt it.

He then turned his attention to the left wall—since in front of him stood a cliff straight and smooth and at least two hundred feet high. Here, on the left, were overhanging ledges bordered with bushes evidently watered from some hidden spring. Shelton surveyed the prospect from a little distance, saw deep shadow under one ledge where there should be sunlight, and rode over there. It was the first place he had seen that looked as if it might be the den of a bear.

Even when he came close it strongly resembled a cave of some sort. Shelton got down, dropped the reins so that Dutch would stand, and clambered over the loose rocks that had rolled down the slope during the centuries past.

He stopped just where the sunlight stopped also and stared at the wide mouth yawning blackly before him. He could look into it for a little way and see how rough were the walls. The floor, once it left the outer edge, was fine, white sand, moist as though a tide had just receded and left it bare.

As Shelton stood gazing down at it, wondering how such white sand got there in that gray country, he saw tracks—a good many of them. Some were long and uncannily human and yet not human—the tracks of the bear. But there were tracks also of a man's boots. Huge boots, that could belong to no one save Alec Burney, of the Sunbeam. Shelton's jaw dropped a little when he saw those and he stared at them a long while before he ever thought of going on.

At last he turned his head and looked back out into the sunlight, blinking from gazing too long upon the blackness. In the open beyond Dutch a hawk was circling slowly with head dropped forward, watching for unwary gophers. It was all very peaceful and very reassuring, and whether he realized it or not, Shelton C. Sherman needed something at that moment stolidly matter-of-fact to steady his reeling fancies.

For Burney was at home, he felt certain of that. And yet these tracks looked fresh. And those other tracks, those huge impressions of feet not quite human, they were fresh also; or so he believed, in his ignorance of the fact that in moist sand which is sheltered from the weather a track will remain fresh-looking for a long while.

He had come prepared to explore a cave if he found one; that is, he had purloined a candle end which he had found in the bunkhouse, and he had plenty of matches. He pulled the bit of candle from his pocket, lighted it and went into the dark like the foolhardy fellow he was. He carried the light in his left hand, however, and in his right he held, tight gripped, the big forty-five six-shooter which Spider had lent him. He was tingling with excitement, his senses a-tiptoe with enthusiasm for the adventure.

Just at first he was obliged to stoop a little and even then his hat crown scraped upon the rough rock ceiling. He thought that Burney, since he really must have come in here, must have bent almost double.

It seemed to be just a long tunnel straight into the hill; an ancient, subterranean outlet for water or lava or something, he did not quite know what. When he held the light down he still saw the tracks of the beast and of the man pointed into the hill. That there were none coming out did not occur to him as being significant until he proceeded for two hundred feet or more. When he did notice it, he took a fresh grip on the six-shooter and went more cautiously.

He was not afraid of Burney—though a growing conviction was upon him that he did not really know Burney after all; not if he were in the habit of appearing to be in two places at once. He knew that he had left the big man at the ranch, his great paws dexterously making bread. And yet he apparently had preceded Shelton into the cave. There was no explaining that feat. But the beast—well, he felt that it was wise to be prepared to shoot at a moment's notice, because a bear of such enormous size might be a pretty tough proposition if a fellow failed to kill him with a first shot or two.

So he went on and on. Once or twice, the light from his candle failed to reach the rock wall upon one side or the other, and he began to wonder if there might not be branches running off in other directions. That possibility made him more cautious still. He tried to follow where the tracks led, which became somewhat difficult, since the floor varied its moist sand covering with a shale rock that left no mark. Still he kept on going.

Finally the tunnel forked, plainly and unmistakably. He could stand before a wedge of sweating rock and look down both fearsome passages, and he hesitated there, flaring the light into one tunnel and then into the other, eagerly looking for some sign of his quarry.

And then, while he stood there undecided, the skin began to creep and prickle at the back of his neck—where the hair of our cave-dwelling ancestors used to rise at the first warning of danger. At first Shelton did not quite know what ailed him, for the sensation was absolutely new to him. Involuntarily he glanced around for some hiding place; just why, he did not know.

Out there in the blackness beyond the farthest candle gleam, something was watching him. It was like the sense of being followed the night before, except that now he was both agitated and alarmed. Without reasoning the thing out, he dodged precipitately into the left-hand passage and ran until his candle blew out with the draft he himself created.

He stopped then and listened, his eyes straining into the darkness out of which he had come. While he fumbled for a match in his pocket, he heard the rapid thump of his own heart, and with it the thin sound of water dripping somewhere. That was all. The rest was impenetrable blackness, like a wall, and silence that was like a velvet curtain hung before it. And yet—

Shelton C. Sherman stood with his back against the wall and knew that he was afraid. He knew that his fear was a blind, unreasoning fear, born perhaps of tricky nerves rebelling against that dark journey into the middle of a mountain. He relighted the candle and knew that its flaring and fading was the fault of his hand which shook so that he could not hold it steady. He felt his heart beating faster and harder, until it almost choked him. But he meant to go on —even his inner panic could not divert him from his purpose.

Then suddenly the terrible silence was split by a scream. Human, it sounded, and yet not human but beastly—horrible. Shelton dropped the candle and dug his free fingers into the rock beside him. For a moment he thought his heart had stopped beating completely. His knees buckled under him so that only the rock at his back supported him. The gun was forgotten in his hand.

And then he heard something running, somewhere, even while the cave was yet horribly playing with the echoes of that scream. Something was running down that other passage with long leaps, as it seemed to him, and with the beat of four padded feet upon the rock floor. Then it must have struck the sand, because the sounds became suddenly muffled and scarcely distinguishable. Indeed, had he not been standing in such a horribly still place, probably he would have heard nothing at all.

Weak, shaking, scared so that his trembling reached the middle of his bones, Shelton pressed his back against the uneven wall behind him and waited; and listened; and glared into the blackness, half expecting to see some terrifying thing take shape before him. He wanted light, yet he was afraid to stoop and grope for the candle, afraid to light a match and look for it, afraid even to move. There was a quick suffocating beat in his throat, a heavy pounding in his chest, and in his brain was a numbness through which he could not think clearly.

Shelton confessed afterward that it took him at least an hour to pull himself together until he had the nerve to find his stub of candle and light it. But he did find it; and he lighted it, with furtive glances around him, when the blaze flamed up and drove the heavy darkness back so that it did not seem to be pressing the very life out of him. What he never told any one was that Spider's gun lay on the ground where he had dropped it in his panic. He picked it up and carried it in his hand again.

He was panting when he came out into the sunlight, though he had not run except the last few rods when he could see the light glimmer ahead of him. He sat down where the sun shone hotly upon the yellow soil, a little way out from the edge, and thanked God for the bright light of day. In a minute he remembered Dutch, standing down the slope with the reins dropped to the ground; anchored, Spider called it.

He stood up and stared this way and that way, shading his eyes with the brim of his hat pulled down. He refused to believe it, but Dutch was gone.

CHAPTER TWELVE

THE SQUAW IN THE CAÑON

SHELTON searched the whole cañon bottom with his eyes. A horse could scarcely hide there, unless he climbed the almost perpendicular sides and got behind the bowlders that jutted out everywhere. Dutch would not do that; he was too lazy. Moreover, he was so thoroughly trained to the dropped reins that he would stand for hours and never stir out of his tracks. He must have gone down the cañon, scared by the thing that came out of the cave.

The thought served to hearten Shelton considerably. There was no shame in being afraid of anything that could scare old Dutch, he told himself. And there was another point; it couldn't have been Burney who came out of the cave, for Dutch would never have been afraid of him; though in spite of the evidence of the fresh boot tracks, Shelton had not yet convinced himself that Burney was ever in that cave.

It was queer. The whole thing was almighty queer, he told himself, when his pulse dropped to normal and fear ceased to cloud his intellect. There were a lot of things which he certainly would never have believed if any of the boys had told him about them; Spider, for instance, or Spooky.

He wished they were both with him now, so that he could prove a few things which were going to sound mighty incredible.

It occurred to Shelton that the tracks coming out of the cave would prove whether it was Burney or the bear—if it really were a bear, which he was beginning to doubt. He had never heard or read of a bear screaming like that. A panther might, perhaps. It had been a shriek, though; a half-human scream that fairly curdled one's blood. He had to admit that he was beginning to lose faith in the bear.

He had forgotten to blow out his candle, but when he looked at it, he saw that the wind had performed the service for him. He glanced behind him at the wide, sinister grin of the cave mouth, debated within himself and, with a hunch of his shoulders, felt in his pocket for a match.

He lit his candle, shielding its blaze from the breeze with fingers creditably steady, considering how terribly he had been scared, and went in again to where the sand was moist and smooth, save where feet had pressed into it the imprint of their passing. He saw his own tracks going in and coming out again, the toes deep printed to prove how fast he'd run, bowed down to avoid the low roof of the tunnel. He shivered a little when he remembered the stark terror that had driven him forward at the last. Then there were the tracks of those two, the beast and the man, going back into the dark. But save his own, there were no tracks coming out.

Shelton forced himself to make sure; forced himself to examine the sand floor closely, from wall to wall. Twice he went across the tunnel, holding the candle close to earth, so interested in the search that he forgot to fear what the dark might hold even then. It was a fact. There were tracks going in; his own and the tracks of Burney and of the beast. There were his own tracks coming out, running—with long strides and the toes pressed deep. And that was absolutely all.

And yet something must have come out of that cave, since Dutch was gone. It would take something very much out of the ordinary to force Dutch's horse instincts above his long years of range training and make him run off of his own accord. To be sure, some one might have ridden him off—but there were no tracks!

61

He came out again and stood in the sunshine, looking down over the sunlit hollow beneath him. His candid blue eyes were clouded with troubled thought. What he ought to do was go back to that fork in the cave and pick up the tracks and follow them. Spider would do that—maybe, if he were not too scared. But his enthusiasm for caves had left him completely. There *was* something back in there. Not only did the tracks prove that, but there was the scream he had heard, and afterward the leaping footsteps running down the black tunnel.

There was something mighty mysterious about the whole thing; Burney's tracks, for one thing. And there were those sheep which Vida had told him about; a dozen or more dead, with their necks twisted in a most unaccountable manner. He could not trace any connection with this cave and the dead sheep, though he felt that there must be one. He could not visualize Burney riding miles in the night just to wring the necks of a dozen or more sheep. The beast that made those tracks and had screamed so horribly might have done it, perhaps. Burney would have to be a madman to commit so wanton a depredation. He could not believe that Burney was mad.

He shook himself free of such fantastic thoughts. The first thing to do was to find Dutch, he told himself; and resolutely set off down the cañon. The familiar world of bright blue sky and drifting white clouds, and the grays and browns and blacks of the surrounding hills seemed never so beautiful as now, after that cave. When he had gone a little distance, he turned and studied the ledges of the hillside. But he could not see where the cave had any other possible opening, so he went on, puzzling over the mystery.

What the deuce could it be that had screamed like that? What kind of animal could run over wet sand and leave no trace behind it? What could Burney have been doing in that cave? And then, who or what had killed those sheep Vida had told him about, and the dog that had been "squashed"?

He was so engrossed in trying to find answers to his own questions that he wandered into a branch of the cañon which he had never seen before. Going up, there had seemed to be no way except the one he traveled; going down, other gorges

62

appeared like the knotted fingers of an opened hand. Into one of these he had blundered, and thought it strange because he found no trace of Dutch, or any opening into the larger cañon, or any rock or turn that looked familiar.

He walked a considerable distance before it occurred to him that this might be a different gorge. Even when he suspected that, he was not alarmed. He still had his compass and the Sunbeam ranch lay west of the Haunted Hills; therefore the mere matter of getting home seemed perfectly simple to an optimistic young fellow who knew nothing much about traveling in such a junk heap of nature's left-overs from mountain building.

He must have traveled for an hour or more without getting anywhere. He was beginning to wonder where he would be apt to strike that first cañon and overtake Dutch, when he saw something on a rock before him. A heap of old clothes, it looked like, and he was struck by the oddity of it. He stopped to examine it curiously from a little distance, then went on more cautiously. Where there were clothes there were likely to be people.

He was quite close when the heap moved and a head, muffled in many grimy folds of some red stuff, swung toward him. Shelton was astonished to find the thing alive. He was more astonished when he discovered the heap to be not only alive, but a woman. A squaw, he knew from the examples he had seen at the railroad stations during the last few hours of his journey west; a squaw old and seamed and shrunken, as if to match the hills.

Shelton went up to her and stood still behind the rock. She appeared to be blind, for her lids were red and gummed almost shut, so that only the tiniest slits of bleary eyes could be seen. Yet she stared at him almost as if she saw him standing there. He did not know quite how to address a creature like this, but the circumstance seemed to demand speech.

"How-de-do?" he began politely. "Do you live around here?"

She continued to stare at him as she shook her head. "No see," she muttered and laid a bony finger to her eyes.

Shelton had read of old crones who muttered and pointed and spoke prophecies in halting sentences like that. It tickled

63

him to have stumbled upon one who measured up to his ideas of what such a creature should be like. This crone certainly looked the part.

"Do you mean you're blind?" he asked.

"No see," she croaked again. "Long time headache—no see."

Shelton never had heard a human voice sound just like that. He sat down upon a near-by rock and fanned himself with his hat. He was pretty tired and it was hot. He eyed the squaw curiously.

"If you're blind, how could you get away out here?" he wanted to know.

"See walk—lilly bit. Long time headache," she murmured, her wizened palm pressed against her forehead. "What yo' name?"

Shelton told her and he added that he was from the Sunbeam ranch. "You know the Sunbeam? You know Mr. Burney's ranch?" he asked her, while he stuffed tobacco into his pipe. His lunch was tied to the saddle on Dutch, wherever that was.

"Me know—Alec—" she muttered, and stopped, her jaws gumming words soundlessly. "Alec—"

"Yes, his name is Alec too—though I didn't know any one ever called him that. You know him? *Big* man!"

"Big, big man—fadder—big man. Die long time. I know. I see Alec—fadder die. Bear—" She waved his skinny hand that was like a mummy's. "Bear kill. I see. Long time. I his woman."

"Oh, say!" Shelton held his pipe sagging between his knees while he stared at her. Of course, he could only guess at what the old thing really meant, and she might be crazy, at that. But still—"You don't mean you're Alec Burney's mother?" he cried, his incredulity showing plainly in his voice.

She shook her head at that, muttering some Indian words. "No, no—Alec mudder—no," she denied. "His woman—Alec —fadder."

Whatever she meant by that, it was practically all that Shelton could get out of her. It seemed to him that her mind was as clouded as her vision, though her taciturnity might

64

be set down to Indian stolidity, or perhaps a shyness in attempting to use the English language.

For a few minutes longer he talked with her, getting vague answers that meant nothing to him. She kept repeating the fact that she had headache long time and that she could only see a "lilly bit." But when he asked her whether there were any great big bears in that country, she muttered Indian words under her breath and appeared to forget that he was there, but scratched at the gravelly soil with a stout stick which she carried, apparently as a staff.

But Shelton was a persistent young man. "Any bears in this country?" He varied the question.

"Long time—big bear kill—" And that was as much as she spoke intelligibly. Shelton thought perhaps she was referring to Burney's father. When he asked her if she meant Alec's father, she shook her head and pointed to the northward.

"Montana," she said quite plainly. "Long time—Alec—lilly boy." Which seemed definite enough, as far as it went.

If she had ever seen any bear in this neighborhood, she managed to conceal the fact. She also seemed to know nothing about any caves. "No see," she would mutter, and point to her eyes, whenever Shelton questioned her concerning that immediate locality. Neither could he discover where she lived or whether she had any family to take care of her.

So presently he left her sitting there, like a bundle of old clothes thrown in a heap upon a rock, and went on down the cañon. Several times he looked back. Had she not been blind, he would have sworn the old hag was watching him craftily, leaning upon the blackened stick clasped in her two claw-like hands. Even when a jutting crag hid her from his sight, his thoughts somehow clung to her with the unpleasant sensation that he had come close to something evil.

By using his compass freely and climbing laboriously over the ridge to his right, he got at last into the cañon he knew. After that he began looking for Dutch without any very cheering prospect of finding him. In the belief that the horse would go home he at last turned his toes toward the Sunbeam and plodded up the bluff to the higher ground, thinking more of his own physical discomfort just then than he did of the bear, whose hide he had wanted for a rug.

65

It was growing dusky again and he was ravenously hungry when he began to feel again that he was being watched and followed; a suspicion which made him forget his appetite and his aching feet and his chagrin at having nothing more than a story to carry home with him.

Once he stopped behind a rock and waited, his gun leveled upon the back trail. He stood there for several minutes and heard nothing, saw nothing. He went on disgustedly, feeling that he had no more time to fool away, if he expected to get home before midnight. Yet as soon as he moved forward he knew that something else moved forward also, following cautiously, watchfully, upon his trail.

Curiously enough, he was not afraid. Perhaps he had exhausted his capacity for fear back there in the cave. Now, he was filled with a baffled sense of anger, because he could neither shake off the feeling nor catch a glimpse of the thing that caused it. As the dark settled down upon the sageland and left him more completely isolated than he had been with the near company of the hills, his mood resembled that of a child who has been teased to a sulky petulance. Yet underneath it was forming a grim determination to run the thing to earth, come what may.

His panic in the cave he called a fluke, a trick played upon him by his nerves. He meant to go back and make a thorough search of the place, and he debated within himself the advisability of trying to enlist the help of the boys. He did not believe they were really afraid of the spook. He did not believe they were afraid of anything on earth, when you came right down to cases. Which goes to prove that Shelton C. Sherman was not after all a fool; he was merely a young man who was growing up faster than he or any one realized, thanks to the rugged life he was living, that threw him more or less upon his own resources.

CHAPTER THIRTEEN
WAS BURNEY HOME LAST NIGHT?

SHELTON dragged his weary bones in the bunkhouse just when the boys were smoking their before-bedtime cigarettes and wondering what had "went with Shep"—using their own vernacular.

"Why, hello, Shep," Spooky greeted him with a very sincere relief in his tone. "We just was talkin' about catching you up and puttin' a bell on yuh. You'll git your brand blotted if you don't quit strayin' off like this." He must have seen then that something was wrong, for he stopped suddenly and eyed Shelton through a haze of cigarette smoke.

Shelton had slumped down upon a bench as if he did not care whether he ever moved again or not. His face was pale under the new coat of sunburn, his eyes were sunken and had purple shadows beneath them, and the muscles of his cheeks sagged with complete physical exhaustion.

Spider looked, yawned and stretched his arms with an ostentatious casualness as he got up from the bed where he had been sprawling luxuriously.

"Better come and lay down, Shep," he suggested carelessly. When Shelton made no move, Spider went over and took him by the arm, much as one would impress obedience upon a sulky child.

"That bunk's a lot more able and willing to hold you up than that pore little bench is," he explained, and led the young man to the bed, pushing him gently down upon it. He pulled a pillow under Shelton's inert head, stooped and lifted his dragging feet and laid them comfortably upon the blankets. Then he pulled his own hat down over his eyebrows and went outside with the same casual manner as he had used from the first. He was back before Spooky and Jim had fairly begun questioning Shelton about his condition and the lateness of his arrival home. Spider carried the coffeepot and a plate of beans and bread. A tin cup hung by its handle from one finger.

"Here, Shep, put yourself outside of some grub," he commanded gruffly. "Coffee's cold, but it'll do the business just the same—seeing you ain't froze."

He poured a cup of the black muddy fluid and compelled Shelton to rise to an elbow and drink every drop. Then he pulled a box close to the bunk, set the plate upon it within easy reach of Shelton's apathetic hand, and sat down negligently upon the other bunk, flicked the ashes off his cigarette, saw that it was cold, and fumbled for a match. "Go ahead and eat," he urged lazily. "Then you can tell us how about it."

Shelton ate a little and then he told "how about it." And the three listened attentively and without banter, while Pike snored raucously from a farther corner of the room. He told of the cave and of the tracks, and Spider leaned with an elbow on either knee, his feet swinging over the side of the bunk, and smoked and stared at the floor as he listened.

He told of his panic of fright and of the scream and of the sound of running in the dark—and Spooky opened his mouth half an inch and let it stay so, and forgot to smoke, while he stared at Shelton's haggard face and listened to the tale. Breed Jim sat with his arms folded Indian-fashion, chewed tobacco mechanically and glanced now and then sidelong at the other two, while he took in every word. And so Shelton's story came down to the old squaw sitting on the rock in the cañon, who manifested such acuteness of hearing while her vision seemed hopelessly blurred—and he told about her also and what she had said about Burney's father.

"That's right," Jim testified stolidly, around his cud. "Burney's father was a squaw man up in Montana. He got clawed up by a grizzly in the Bitter Root country when Burney was a kid. I thought the old woman was dead long ago. She had a kid by old man Burney. A feller that prospected up in the Bitter Root Mountains told me about it. The kid died, or was killed somehow, I don't recollect which. I'm pretty sure he told me the old woman was dead too."

"Well, she isn't, apparently; but the first strong wind is likely to blow her away," said Shelton. "She looked like a bat dressed up as a scarecrow and her mind is certainly wobbly." And he went on with the story.

"And say, fellows," he said earnestly, when he had described his long tramp home and how he had been followed again by something he never got to see, "there's something

68

mighty strange behind all this. I don't know what kind of a beast it is, but I'm going to make it my business to find out. I can't somehow believe that Burney killed those sheep—"

"What sheep?" interjected Spider, lifting his head for the first time since Shelton began to talk.

"Why, the Williams sheep. Vida told me about it. A lot of their sheep were killed last night, over the other side of that long ridge of the Haunted Hills, where her uncle is camped with a band. And say, fellows, their necks were wrung, she said. And one of the dogs—she called him Laddie —ran out; and he was killed also. She said that it had been 'squashed,' so that its ribs were broken, and its neck twisted like the sheep. Can you beat that?

"She thinks Burney did it. She says he's the only one in the country strong enough—and of course, that's true as far as it goes. But I think it was that bear I saw the tracks of."

"A bear," Spooky asserted, "wouldn't hardly kill sheep like that. He might come into a band and pack off one or two, and he might go through a band, just cuffin' 'em right and left, like that." Spooky illustrated with thrashing arms. "He'd break their necks, I reckon, if he done that—or cave in their ribs or something. But it don't look natural, him grabbin' every sheep separate and wringin' its neck. That looks to me more—human." Spooky spoke with a certain reluctance, sending an inquiring glance toward Spider.

"Didn't anybody see it or tracks, or—?" Jim stopped to turn his tobacco cud.

"The sheep would tromp out any tracks," Spider told him shortly, shifting his position a little without looking up. There was a certain warped board in the floor which he appeared to find absorbingly interesting.

"Yeah,—that's right," assented Jim.

"Well, Vida said her uncle ran out and got a glimpse of him going off over a little hill, where he was outlined against the sky." Shelton unconsciously lowered his voice and glanced toward the door. "She says her uncle would swear it was Burney. She said a person couldn't make any mistake in a man like him. But still—" his head dropped back wearily on the pillow—"I stick to the bear theory. A bear would go

69

off on its hind legs, wouldn't it, if it were carrying a sheep?"

"It might. Probably it would," Spooky agreed with evident relief. "Yeah, come to think of it, I guess it would."

"Well, I say it was that bear—or whatever animal it is, fellows. And I'm going to keep on hunting till I get it. They think over there that Burney did it—"

"Burney was home all last night, wasn't he?" Spooky asked aggressively of no one in particular. "How could it be him?"

Spider cocked one eye in the direction of Spooky, lifted one eyebrow, but said never a word. His look asked the other how they could know whether Burney was at home or not. He slept at the cabin alone, more than fifty yards from the bunk house. They had no way of checking his movements. As a matter of fact, it could very easily be Burney, and each one of the four knew that it could. More than that, they knew that it probably was Burney. Even to Shelton, had he admitted it, the bear theory seemed a little far-fetched.

Still, it did not seem like Alec Burney to sneak into a sheepman's band and kill sheep by stealth in that fashion. Burney would fight, as his men well knew; but always he had fought in the open and had seemed to prefer that the odds should be against him, if there were odds. The very bigness of him and the strength of him had always made him slow to take action. And the Williams sheep had not yet injured the Sunbeam range; nor had the Williams men done anything that might be construed as the beginning of hostilities.

True, they were crowding close—too close to be welcome neighbors—and Burney had ridden over and told them so. That much was perfectly logical, understandable—right and just, according to range ethics. But to come that same night and kill sheep under the very nose of Jake Williams, and to sneak away afterward in the dark—that was something at which even the Sunbeam cowboys balked.

Their talk dwindled after that. Once or twice Shelton wondered what could have become of old Dutch and Spooky told him that they would hunt him up to-morrow. Spider went out and stayed for a long time. When he returned, he threw his hat down as if it had displeased him, and had no more

70

than a grunt for Spooky, who showed a disposition to talk.

Shelton lifted his head and looked in Spider's direction for a minute. "Say, Spider, come over here and let me whisper in your ear," he said, with his old, boyish tone. "I've got a sweet little message that nobody but you must hear. Come on—I promised her."

Spider paused in the act of pulling off a boot and eyed Shelton crossly. Then he caught a significant lowering of an eyelid, dropped the boot and went and bent over Shelton, his ear close to Shelton's lips. And that young man, instead of giving a message, asked one question. Spider's light blue eyes looked steadily into Shelton's for a second before he answered and the lurking little devil in them changed to a gleam of steel.

"Gone!" he whispered in reply and went back and took off the other boot.

Two in that cabin slept little that night and even Spooky was inclined to lie awake and wonder what was the mystery of the Haunted Hills.

CHAPTER FOURTEEN

VIDA'S ON THE WARPATH

VIDA WILLIAMS, hard of eye and lips, hot from fast riding and looking ready to fight the whole Sunbeam outfit, rode up to the cabin and pulled her right foot out of the stirrup, ready to dismount. But when she saw Spider and Shelton coming toward her from the stable—they having seen her gallop by—she stayed in the saddle and waited grimly until they came up.

"Where's Goliath?" she demanded shortly, with no greeting whatever.

"In the cabin, I think. Good morning, Miss Vida. Will you meet—well, Spider is the only name that I know belongs to him. This is Miss Williams, Spider."

Miss Williams gave Spider a nod and a glance far from cordial. "I want to see Goliath and I want to see him quick," she said. "I wish you'd call him out."

Spider went at once to the cabin and opened the door.

71

"There's a lady wants to see you, Burney," he called within and turned back.

Shelton was asking Vida what was the matter and wouldn't she get off her horse and rest a while. And Vida was giving him short answers that told him nothing except that her mood was anything but friendly and her time was limited.

Bending his shoulders forward to save his head a bump, Burney appeared in the doorway, stared at Vida for a minute with his little, deep-set, twinkling eyes, and came toward her. He was so big that Vida's horse was afraid of him, and when he saw that, he stopped and came forward more slowly. Within ten feet of her he stood still. Their eyes were nearly on a level when they looked at each other.

"You wanted to see me?" he asked her in his surprisingly high, light voice.

"I wanted to ask you what's your object in killing off our sheep the way you're doing," Vida stated harshly, not one whit abashed by the size of him. "I've come over to tell you, Mr. Goliath, that if you kill another sheep of ours, I'm going to watch my chance and plant a bullet where it'll do the most good. You aren't easy to miss, you know!"

"I ain't killed any sheep of yours," Burney denied, reddening under her angry gaze. "I didn't know there'd been any sheep killed. When was it done?"

"You needn't try to make me believe you don't know! Or maybe you were walking in your sleep last night and night before last," she said contemptuously. "Who else in the country but you could grab up a sheep and break its neck, and crack its ribs just by squeezing it? Night before last it was Uncle Jake's band and last night it was ours. And last night you killed twenty before I could get out where I could take a shot at you. Big as you are, I missed you in the dark—"

"It wasn't me," Burney told her again, his little eyes fixed upon her face in a steady stare. "I've never been near your camp except the other day—in the morning. I told your father to keep away from Piute Hills. If you're sensible, you'll get your father to move his sheep back the other way."

"We're not going to move and you can't make us!" Vida's voice sharpened to a hysterical note. "Poppy might get scared out because he hates to have trouble with any one, but I won't

72

let him move. It's fortunate that I happened to be out here with him when all this started. We'll fight you as long as we've got a sheep left standing on four feet.

"That's open range over there and we've as much right to it as any one. You needn't think you can hog all the grass in the country, and you needn't think you can come sneaking into our band at night and kill sheep until you're tired, and not get some of your own medicine. I—oh, I wish I could just take *you* and wring your neck the way you did to the sheep!" Tears of rage were in her voice. "Just because you're big as all outdoors, you needn't think you can run us out—"

Burney took a step nearer and the horse shied away. He stopped and the crimson had left his face so that he looked actually pale.

"Miss Williams, I never killed your sheep. I don't want to have any trouble with your father unless he drives me to it. I ain't a quarrelsome man when I'm left alone. I bought your father out once, but I can't afford to do it again—I lost money on the deal before. I lost a lot of money. And I can't afford to lose no more.

"Miss Williams, I'm in debt up to the hilt, as it is. I've got to make my cattle pull me out or else I'm liable to go under. And it ain't fair for your father to bring in sheep on me. You know how quick a range can be sheeped out, and there ain't any too much for my own stock. I—I don't want to act mean about it, but—you better talk your father into moving back further—"

"I will not!" Vida refused to be impressed by Burney's apologetic manner, which so astonished Spider and Shelton. "We're in just as bad a fix as you are—and there are three of us to think of and only one of you. We're in debt ourselves and we've got to make the sheep pull us out. We need the range as badly as you do. You know very well that the feed is poor back toward Pillar Butte and we're not going to change our range for you or anybody else.

"I said before, and I want you to remember it, every one of you; if you kill another single, solitary sheep, I'll shoot you myself—in daylight, when I won't miss." She swung her horse away from the giant with a reckless laugh. "So if it's war you want, go to it. I'm not a man, but if I take a hand in this killing game, you'll think I'm a dozen. But I'm not like you, Mr. Burney," she flung over her shoulder. "I don't sneak up on people after dark. I'll fight in the daylight. And remember—if you kill any more of our sheep, I'll kill you. I'll take my chance with a jury."

She looked at Shelton, flicked Spider with a careless glance and gave a defiant lift of her chin, though her cheeks reddened under their surprised stares.

"I mean it!" she bolstered her pride and her anger. "I suppose you think it isn't ladylike for me to come over here and talk this way, but I can't help that. It's more important to be human and stand by my own father. And if any one in our outfit has got to wade in and fight, I'd rather be the one. I'd stand more show in court, if it came to that."

"Making capital out of your sex?" Shelton reproved mildly. "You wouldn't do that, Miss Vida!"

"Oh, wouldn't I?" Vida curled her lip at him in a way to crimple his vanity. "Why not? Women never do get a square deal, anyway. You men don't show any squeamishness about making capital of our sex, do you? You take every advantage of us that you can get. So when we know where to hit your weak points, I believe in aiming at them. And if it came to working a bunch of mutts in the jury box in order to get justice, you can bet your hat I'd work them to a fare-you-well. Men are the limit, anyway."

She laughed at him in a way to redden his whole face. "Look at you, for instance. You'd like to flirt a little with me, just because you're lonesome and I'm the only girl in the country. You wouldn't give a whoop for my feelings, just so you were entertained. And do you call that fair? Isn't that making capital out of my sex?

"And Mr. Burney, here. Just because he's big and strong and can lord it over common men, he thinks I don't count. Just because I'm a girl, he passes me up as if I didn't have any interest in those sheep over there. Oh, you all—every darn one of you—you think, because I'm a girl, all I can do is talk! Well, you just go ahead the way you started out and see!" She sent a cold, gray glance around the group, letting it dwell longest on Shelton's bewildered face. Then, with another little, defiant toss of her head, she struck her horse down the rump with her quirt and rode away from the Sunbeam ranch with the superb grace of perfect horsemanship, which only comes to those born to the saddle. The three watched her in dead silence until she was out of sight.

"She'd shoot, all right—b'lieve me!" Spider commented, when she was no more than a bobbing black speck against the sunlit sage.

"I never killed their damn sheep," Burney muttered defensively. "But if they keep crowding up on my range—" He turned sullenly and went back into the cabin, leaving the two standing there to think what they pleased.

"Well, come on, Shep. Let's get out after Dutch." Spider turned away toward the stables. "Looks to me like things are beginning to tighten. You've got a regular girl there, boy; one that'll take some living up to."

But Shelton declined to enter into a discussion of Vida Williams just then. He fell into pace beside Spider and walked for some rods before he spoke.

"Shall we take candles?" he asked then, as if nothing had happened to interrupt their plans.

"Sure, we'll take candles. Might as well make a clean sweep, Shep, and give that cave a thorough goin' over; that is, if you ain't scared to go back."

"I want to go, whether I'm scared or not," Shelton declared firmly. "I'd rather face whatever it is and fight it out than spend the rest of my life wondering what it is. Oh, shucks!" he added with sudden impatience. "What's the use of hedging? Vida's made a big mistake if she thinks I'm just flirting with her. What do you think of the stand she took? Pretty nervy for a girl to face Burney that way, don't you think? She certainly has got courage—"

"Yeah. Skate a little closer, Shep. We might as well talk about it now as any time. What about them sheep?"

Shelton, however, did not care to skate over that particular bit of thin ice. He said he didn't know and changed the subject. Whereat Spider grinned to himself and then became much occupied with his own thoughts.

"Well, right over behind that cut-off butte is the cañon

where I found the cave," Shelton drew up on the east side of a pinnacle and pointed ahead. "We can get down into the big cañon—"

"Yeah, I know that big one. I've been in it. That's where I was trailing a lion when—something commenced to foller me." Spider cupped his palms around a match blaze. "Might have been a lynx," he conceded, when his cigarette was lighted and he had blown out the match. "These hills is full of animals a man never sees."

— "I been thinking maybe it was a lynx you heard in the cave; or a lion. They let out an ungodly squall sometimes. Didn't you happen to notice any round tracks, like a great big cat? Tracks about that big, say?" With his bent fingers he enclosed a circle larger than a cup and watched Shelton's face hopefully.

"No. But I did see a bear's track. You don't believe me now, but you will when I show you. And I saw Burney's tracks too," he added doggedly.

"I don't know why Burney wouldn't have as much license to go into a cave as you have," Spider observed dryly.

"Well, I suppose he has. But I tell you frankly, I don't like the attitude Burney has been taking. Leave the sheep out of it. I still don't like the way Burney warns other people away from here—and then comes himself on the sly." His jaw squared as suspicion crystallized in his mind. "On second thoughts, I won't leave the sheep out of it. I think those three dozen sheep that have been so mysteriously killed are going to take a lot of explaining."

"And that's why," said Spider calmly, "I'm going to ride over that way and take a look-see for myself. No telling which way Dutch went, seeing he didn't come back to the ranch—and that's mighty funny too. I can't figure out why he never come home. Unless he was rode off—and according to your story, you was the only one down in there except that blind squaw, and she was over in the next cañon.

"Darn it," Spider went on, in a tone of complete bafflement, "there ain't one solitary fact that lines up with any other fact. That's what gets me. You saw bear tracks in that cave and then you heard something *scream*, you say; and only a mountain lion or a lynx would screech out like that.

The girl says Burney killed their sheep like a gorilla had got into the band. And Burney ain't the sheep-killin' kind, if I know anything about him—and I've worked for him over two years now.

"Burney says he never went near their camp except one morning, and any of us would have swore he's been staying right on the ranch for the last few days—and yet he was gone last night. I got up about one o'clock, after I'd missed him outa the cabin and got to thinkin' about it in the night. And his horse and saddle was missing. I went down again at three and they was there. I can't figure out any errand that would take him out all night. And I never knowed Burney to lie. Gosh! He's so ungodly big he don't *have* to lie. What he says goes, around this country, and always has.

"And to pile the agony up still higher, what's become of Dutch? There ain't no reason in the world why he wouldn't come straight on home if he was scared off from where you left him. And he never showed up. Oh, hell!" exclaimed Spider, lifting his hat and settling it on his head at a new angle. "Come on, Shep. Let's go take a look at them sheep for a starter. I think I know about where old Williams will be camped. After that, we'll go take a look at your cave."

CHAPTER FIFTEEN

CALL IT A BEAR TRACK

To look at the dead sheep was a simple matter. The Williams camp had moved since daylight, but when Shelton and Spider saw the white-topped wagon crawling in leisurely fashion up near the hills of sinister repute, and farther away the slowly drifting patch of gray which they knew to be the band of sheep, they had only to swing in on the trail and follow it back to where Spider knew there was a spring.

There they found the dead sheep, lately skinned for their pelts and left to fatten the coyotes. Spider forced his horse close to the fly-blackened carcasses and sat there staring down with frowning brows. Every sheep's neck had been dislocated, and nearly every one had been squeezed flat—

squashed, as Vida had called it. It was not a pretty sight.

Spider lifted his head and studied the low ridges and correspondingly shallow gullies of that vicinity. He scowled again at the skinned carcasses, chewing his underlip in deep thought. He looked across at Shelton, who was hovering agitatedly in the immediate background, because of his horse's violent dislike of dead sheep, and he hunched his shoulders and rode away, back in the direction from which they had come.

"Well, what was it? A bear?" Shelton quizzed him after an expectant silence.

"Ask the sheep," Spider made laconic answer, and added, "They can tell you as much about it as I can."

"But what do you *think* it was?" Shelton, remember, was the persistent type of individual.

"Me, I'm thinkin' damns, right now," said Spider.

Shelton did not cover himself with glory that day. To begin with, he could not find the cañon that ended in the crude amphitheater where the cave was located. He led Spider into two blind pockets in the hills, and in each instance he discovered, after a prolonged search, that it was not the right cañon.

He persisted in riding with too loose a rein, in spite of Spider's repeated warnings and profane instructions, and the horse shied unexpectedly and violently and threw Shelton into a patch of brush. Then it bolted while Shelton thrashed around in there, trying to get out. Spider chased the horse a quarter of a mile over some nasty rocks and washouts before he caught him and led him back, and one can easily guess what his temper was like after that.

Since he was unable to find the cañon which held the cave, Shelton was also unable to discover the gulch in which he had seen the old squaw. In falling, he had scraped the skin off one forearm and had hurt his knee so that he found walking painful, and he was not enthusiastic over riding much farther on that strange horse. The sun blazed down upon them more pitilessly than it had done on any day that spring, which furnished reason enough for the sulky silence that held the two at last.

Then, just when they were picking their way gingerly

across a steep side hill, to where a bare ridge gave promise of a precarious trail into the cañon they must cross if they would reach the Sunbeam without riding an extra ten miles, Spider's sharp eyes caught a glimpse of something moving along the opposite side of the cañon. He pulled up and stared sharply, shading his eyes with his hand.

"What's that, over there?" cried Shelton excitedly, following Spider's gaze.

"You can search me," grunted Spider and rode on.

"It looked to me like a bear," Shelton volunteered, when he overtook Spider. "Or else maybe it was a cow. Did you see it go behind those rocks?"

Spider grunted again and left Shelton to interpret the sound as he pleased. It was not until they descended into the cañon bottom that Spider was surprised into speech. They came full upon Dutch, feeding dispiritedly upon the scanty grass there, and Dutch had neither saddle nor bridle upon him, but only the marks of cruelly hard riding, and a twisted rope that hobbled his front feet so that he must hop laboriously, if he would move at all.

Spider got off his horse and went up closely and examined the hobbles. He straightened, gazed slowly all about him and pushed back his hat from his perspiring forehead.

"Well, I'll be damned!" he said, in a helpless kind of way, and squatted on his heels that he might pick the knots loose and free poor Dutch. His face was a study in mystification.

"Oh, say! Somebody's been trying to steal him!" Shelton exclaimed, looking on. "What is that stuff, Spider? It certainly isn't rope, is it?"

Spider stood up with the thongs in his hand. He looked from them to Shelton and back again, a worried expression in his eyes.

"Don't yuh know what that is?" he asked, more humanly than he had spoken for three full hours. "That there is a strip cut from a fresh sheep pelt. Look there. See how the wool has been hacked off with a knife."

Shelton stared blankly before a gleam of understanding came into his face. "The sheep killer stole him," he declared. "He couldn't get far with his feet tied together," he added, "so there ought to be tracks of the killer around

79

here. Don't you suppose we might get a clue that way?"

"Yeah, I expect we might."

With that encouragement, Shelton dismounted awkwardly, because of his knee, and went limping back and forth where the soil gave promise of receiving and holding tracks. It was Spider who first discovered a trace and he puzzled over the marks—three tracks close beside a crumbling washout where the bank was sandy. Shelton limped up to the spot and gave a small whoop of triumph.

"Oh, say!" he jubilated. "That's the bear whose track I saw the other day. If we could just follow it—"

Spider turned and looked at him. "You sure are an observative cuss," he made dry comment. "Take another look at them three tracks. How high do you figure a bear would have to be to step as long as that?" He placed one foot beside the first track and stepped out toward the next. Spider was not a small man by any means, yet his longest stride fell short of the second bear track.

Shelton watched him and grasped his meaning. "Then what the deuce do you think it is, if it isn't a bear?" he demanded, when Spider stood off with his hands on his hips, staring again at the unbelievable tracks. The cowboy looked at him, started to speak, then hesitated.

"Oh, go on and tell me," Shelton urged, with some impatience. "I'm not a child, and I don't think I'm altogether a fool, even if I do let myself go and act that way sometimes." His face became suddenly mature and competent looking. "I've got to get at the bottom of this thing, you know. I can't leave Vida to fight it out alone, and that precious father and uncle of hers don't seem to be much force. What is it you suspect?"

Spider drew his tongue along his lower lip. "Well, just between you and me and the gatepost, Shep, I'll tell yuh what I think. What I know, for that matter. It's a man trying to make out like he's a bear. Wearing some kinda bear fixin's on his feet to hide his own tracks. Makin' a damn poor stagger at it too, if you ask me." He gave a snort of contempt. "He plumb forgot to step short, for one thing, and then his feet was too big."

Shelton gave Spider a long look, then stared down at the

tracks. Presently he followed Spider's example. He placed his foot alongside the first track and measured the stride. He was six feet and two inches tall, with a stride much longer than Spider's. Yet he was obliged to step as far as he could reach in order to place his foot alongside the second track. He looked up.

"Well, there's only one man—"

With a stern gesture Spider stopped him. "Some things is better off inside your head," he said bluntly. "We can't help what we think, Shep, but we needn't go around shooting off our faces about it. Call it a bear track and let it go at that. I ain't going to build up a case on a few marks in the sand and you ain't, either." He glanced moodily toward Dutch. "We've found what we was hunting. Let's be drifting toward home."

But first he stopped and scraped the edge of his boot sole carefully over the tracks until they were quite obliterated. After that he took his rope and tied an end around the neck of the brown horse which Shelton had been riding.

"I guess you might as well ride Dutch back," he observed. "You're a heap safer on him and Dutch is tough. He can pack you in, all right." And he changed the saddle quickly, as if he were in haste to be gone.

While they rode up out of the cañon and across the level flat, Shelton studied the mystery that had taken hold of them all and forced them out of the careless routine of their days. "What I can't see," he said abruptly, "is what object he'd have. Aside from scaring off Williams and his sheep, it looks—well, childish to go around the country doing things like that."

"I don't know," quelled Spider, "as you're expected to see any object in it. I don't know as any one is."

That did not settle the other's desire to put the puzzle into speech, however. "Well, it certainly doesn't account for my being followed—"

"If you was followed."

"Nor that screaming and running in the cave—"

"If you didn't just lay down somewhere and go to sleep and dream all that cave stuff."

"Oh, say!" Shelton protested. "What do you think I am?"

81

"Aw," Spider cried impatiently, "can't yuh take a hint, Shep? The less said about this thing the better, till we know something of where we're at. Burney's my boss. I've knowed him for more than two years. The best we can do is keep this thing under our hats. We found Dutch and he'd got hung up in the brush somewhere and shucked his saddle. You bein' a tenderfoot, you don't know how to tie a latigo, anyway, so it won't come undone. Let it lay, Shep. Let it lay."

There was little conversation between them after that. They rode slowly down the hill and up to the high pole corral beside the stable. As they dismounted, Burney himself came out of the corral, carrying his saddle in one hand.

"I've got to go to Pocatello," he told them. "I may not be back for three or four days. You kinda keep things moving, Spider." Then he seemed to notice Dutch for the first time. "Oh, yuh found him," he said, with lukewarm interest. "Where was he at?"

"Over in the Haunted Hills," said Spider distinctly, looking up into Burney's little, twinkling eyes. "In a gulch, hobbled with a strip of sheep hide. We couldn't find the saddle and bridle."

For a moment Burney seemed to tower above the two. Then he turned away sharply toward his own horse. "Some of them sheep herders caught him up, most likely," he said. "Might as well let the saddle go; didn't amount to much—and we don't want to have no more trouble with 'em if we can help it.

"Don't want any trouble with anybody," they heard him muttering, while he threw the saddle on his big brown horse. "The girl's crazy, if she thinks I killed her sheep."

He swung into the saddle, and without farewell or further orders, he rode away, a heroic figure of the desert country, straight-backed and straight-legged, the big horse carrying him down the road at a jog trot. The two at the corral stared curiously after him.

CHAPTER SIXTEEN

"HE KILLED UNCLE JAKE!"

B URNEY had not yet returned from Pocatello; indeed, he had been gone not much longer than twenty-four hours, when Vida Williams came riding again to the Sunbeam; riding a heaving flanked, sweat-roughened pony and looking harder of lip and eyes than before.

Spooky had just called to the boys to "come and get it" —meaning supper—and he stood now in the cabin doorway with his hands on his hips, waiting for them to appear. Then came Vida, galloping straight down the trail from the hills, not deigning to pull up or turn aside when she overtook Shelton and Spider and Breed Jim. The boys were obliged to duck out of her way. They came on in the cloud of dust kicked up by her pony's flying heels.

She swung down from her horse and walked purposefully toward Spooky in the doorway. Her sunburned braid of hair was roughened in the wind. Her denim riding skirt was stained with her pony's sweat. Her face was pale under her tan, so that the little freckles on her nose stood out plainer than Shelton had ever seen them, and her eyes held the light of battle. A six-shooter swung at one slim hip, and as she neared the cabin she jerked the gun from its holster and held it hanging at her side. And when they saw that, the boys broke into a trot, hurrying to the door.

"Where's Burney?" she asked, more quietly than one would expect from the look of her, though it was the tense quiet that spells danger.

"Burney's in Pocatello," Spooky volunteered, before Shelton could more than open his mouth. "He went yesterday. Left right after dinner."

"You lie!" Vida flung the words at him as a driver flicks his lash. Her breath was coming quickly and unevenly through flared nostrils. She was forcing herself to be calm and it was not easy, as they could plainly see.

"Where is he?" she demanded fiercely. "You may as well produce him, for I'll get him anyway." She eyed the Sunbeam cowboys with a wary hostility, as if she expected some overt act and was on her guard against it.

Shelton stepped up to her side, laid a hand upon her shoulder and turned to face the three Sunbeam men. Though he did not speak, the action served notice that he was with Vida, whatever the consequences.

Spider looked from him to the girl. "Burney ain't here," he said mildly. "Shep can tell you he left yesterday."

Vida looked from one to the other, met blank questioning in every pair of eyes that stared back at her, and pushed her gun back into its holster. She bit her lip, fighting for control. "He didn't go to Pocatello," she declared, in a strained, hard voice. "He was over on the east side of Piute Hills about three hours ago. He—killed Uncle Jake!" Her voice broke on that last sentence.

"No! You don't—"

"He did! He—oh, Shelton, that man is a fiend!" One hand went up, touching his shoulder. Shelton's arm slipped around her waist. The wordless championship helped her to pull herself together. "I don't blame you boys—I don't suppose you had anything to do with it, but I came here—all keyed up to kill Burney—"

Spider took a step nearer the two. "Let's get this straight, Miss Williams," he said, with a quiet earnestness more impressive than violence. "We don't know a thing about it. All we know is, Burney said he had to go to Pocatello yesterday. We s'posed he'd gone."

"Well, that was just a blind, then, because this afternoon —I think it must have been early—Uncle Jake was herding a band of ewes and lambs on that long slope running out from the big hill, and he was killed"—her eyes widened with the horror of it—"just like the sheep have been killed."

She caught her breath, pressed one hand against her eyes and went on as if she were anxious to tell the thing and be done with it. "He was just grabbed—from behind, I guess— and—his neck was twisted. Just like the sheep."

Spider took a step toward her. "Girl, are you sure of that?" His face was stern.

"Would I be over here if I weren't? Of course it's the truth. I—I saw him. His head was twisted way around over
84

his shoulder." She shuddered and moved closer within Shelton's embrace. "And Uncle Jake's pretty strong, himself, but he didn't have a ghost of a show."

The four of them stared at her incredulously. The thing was too monstrous to grasp all at once. "Killed!" said Shelton, just above his breath. "Why, say! That's murder!"

Vida shivered again and caught her lip between her teeth.

"Wasn't there any sign of a scuffle?" asked Spooky. "Didn't anybody see it happen?"

"No, he was out alone, with just the one dog," Vida explained, stepping away from Shelton, as if she had just now realized the possible significance of his sheltering arm.

"Poppy and I rode over to see him, because some more of our sheep were killed last night, and we wanted to see if Uncle Jake had been bothered, and what he thought we better do about it. Poppy wanted to swear out a complaint against Burney, but he wanted to talk with Uncle Jake about it first. And—we found him—like that. It must have just happened. He—he wasn't cold yet."

"Wasn't there any tracks, or anything?"

"No, there wasn't a sign of anything. He just laid there like he'd been thrown down again. It was on a little rocky ridge. I suppose he had been sitting on the ridge where he could watch the sheep and Burney crawled up on him from behind. He could, easily enough; it's all a web of small ridges and washouts there, where the water has gullied out the side hill. And Burney—"

"What makes you keep on sayin' Burney?" Spooky asked her aggressively.

"Who else but Burney could have done that?" she countered. "Could *you* grab a man the size of Uncle Jake and twist his neck clear around until you broke it? It isn't easy to do, I should think."

"No," Spider soberly agreed, "it ain't easy to do. At the same time—"

"Who else would want to?" she pressed the argument. "Uncle Jake never had any trouble around here with any one except Burney. And you know he's been trying his best to drive us off, ever since we brought our sheep over this side of Pillar Butte."

85

She bit her lips again and fingered the sagging gun belt. Her blind rage was cooling with speech and the unspoken sympathy of these four, and she seemed almost reluctant to go on with the discussion. She was growing more normal —more like the Vida Williams whom Shelton had met out on the high stretches of the Piute foothills. But there was more and she forced herself to speak of it.

"That isn't all," she said. "I *know* he killed Uncle Jake. I can take you over there and show you the proof. I didn't see him do it; no one did. But I saw his tracks down in the gully, right behind the outcropping of rock where Uncle Jake was sitting. It's as plain as print."

"You just said there wasn't no tracks," Spider reminded her bluntly.

"Not up on the ridge, no. It's too rocky up there, and there wasn't a sign of anything, just as I said. But I rode back down in the gully—probably a hundred yards or more beyond where Uncle Jake was. That's where the tracks are, pointing up toward the ridge. Huge boot tracks; Burney's tracks, just the same as he makes around here. There isn't another man in the country with feet the size of his, is there?"

There was no need to answer her question. They knew there was not another man in the country with feet the size of Burney's.

"I guess we better ride over," Spider suggested, after an uneasy silence. "If Burney didn't go to Pocatello, we can easy find it out; a man like him ain't goin' to be overlooked, in town or anywhere else. And if he done what you think he done—"

Spider stopped short and when he continued it was from a new angle of thought. "I've knowed him a long while," he said, "and I've never knowed a thing against him. I never knowed him to harm a livin' soul. And he ain't mean around horses; that's where the brute in a man crops out, generally. At the same time, you never do know all that's in a man."

He turned challengingly toward Spooky. "I can't hardly believe it was Burney," he said. "At the same time, I ain't goin' to back any low-down play like choking a man to death just because he owns a bunch of sheep," he stated flatly.

"I don't care whether it's Burney or my own brother."

"Same here, Pete," Breed Jim shifted his cud to say diffidently, because of the girl's presence.

"Well, come on and eat, seeing it's ready," urged Spooky. "There ain't no use in startin' out with an empty stomach and a few minutes more or less won't make no difference now. If they's tracks," he said to Vida, "we'll foller 'em up. You better come in and have something to eat."

Vida looked into the cabin and shuddered. "I—couldn't," she said disconsolately. But she sat upon a box near the door and drank a cup of hot coffee which Shelton brought out to her.

"I just couldn't go in there," she apologized to him in an undertone. "It's like the den of some wild beast. I—I keep seeing Uncle Jake. And I can't help thinking how Burney must have looked, creeping up that ridge behind him."

"Oh, say! You'll have to cut that out," Shelton protested, somewhat awkwardly. "You've been so brave and nervy all along, it makes me feel ashamed of myself. You mustn't lose your grip now, you know. You're got to put those things out of your mind. Say, I'm going to bring our supper out here and you've got to eat with me. Spooky's a good cook and I always did like to eat in the open air."

Which won a smile from Vida and served to ease the situation.

CHAPTER SEVENTEEN

KILLED LIKE THE SHEEP

THE SUN was low when they rode away from the Sunbeam ranch. Close grouped and silent, they climbed the hill and galloped straight away through the sage and lava rocks toward where the Haunted Hills hunched their black shoulders against the sky. Grim of lip and somber-eyed, they hurried out to look upon the telltale footprints which branded their boss a murderer of the foulest type.

Still ignorant of the circumstances which had planted in the minds of Shelton and Spider the seeds of distrust, Spooky and Breed Jim were inclined to be incredulous still. They would have to see those tracks themselves before they would believe that Burney had been anywhere near the spot.

Shelton and Spider rode with the girl between them, watching the trail as they neared the hills. They did not talk much. When Shelton did attempt a desultory conversation with Vida, trying to divert her thoughts from the tragedy, she answered him only with monosyllables or a shake of the head. Her eyes were frequently blurred with tears and her lips were trembling. For although her Uncle Jake had been an utterly commonplace individual for whom she had felt no very definite affection, nevertheless he was her uncle and he had helped to fill the loneliness of her days.

She had lately looked upon him dead, and now that the first shock of horror had passed, she was feeling the sorrow of a personal loss. It was not until they had crossed the big ridge and were riding down the slope beyond that she turned voluntarily to Shelton.

"You mustn't mind if Poppy seems pretty much on the warpath," she said abruptly. "He's terribly worked up over this and he blames the whole Sunbeam outfit. He swore he'd shoot the first one of you that he got sight of. But he won't really do it. Poppy—just talks like that. He never really does anything."

Unconsciously she had revealed where lay the heaviest weight of responsibility for the family's welfare. Her own slim shoulders drooped under their burden. Her tone betrayed the fact that she was stronger than her father, who "just talked like that." She would have fought, and fought hard, in defense of their property and their rights. Her Poppy talked.

Sensing this, Shelton turned and looked at her compassionately. In the dusk his hand went out and clasped her arm.

"Don't you worry," he said, so low that the others could not hear. "This is all new to me and I'm afraid I'm not much good, but I'll stand by you to the last ditch, Vida. You know that."

"I know you will, Shep," she said simply, turning her face toward him. Her eyes were lustrous with unshed tears. She did not pull her arm away. "I—I don't feel so alone as I did a few hours ago."

Shelton's fingers slid down her arm, clasped her hand closely for a minute, and let it go. In this wise did he take the oath of fealty, and none but Vida knew anything about it; not even Spider, who rode alongside her and seldom missed anything.

It was dark long before they reached the gruesome slope where the body of Jake Williams lay just where it had fallen. A campfire blazed up into the dark beside a near-by ledge, and as the flames leaped and then flickered low, the figure of a man flared into sharp outline and merged again into the shadows.

As they rode closer, they saw him lift his head and listen, looking their way. He had a rifle and with a menacing gesture he pointed it toward them. The firelight must have blinded him, however; for he stood up and craned, then suddenly ducked back into the shadows beyond the light of the flames. A spurt of fire and the sharp crack of his rifle showed how he had mentally placed the newcomers, but the bullet sang its song of flight high over their heads.

"You stop that shooting! It's only the boys I brought with me!" Vida kicked her horse with the spurs and plunged ahead of the others into the firelight which bathed her in its golden glow. "Put down that gun and come in out of the dark!" she commanded impatiently, in the tone one uses toward a mischievous boy. "There's nothing to be scared of. Has Pete got back yet?"

"No." Her father came reluctantly forward, his bushy beard quite concealing any emotion his face might otherwise have revealed. "Who are these men?" he challenged.

"They're some boys from the Sunbeam ranch. They came over to do what they can to help. They want to look around and try and pick up the tracks. But it's pretty dark for that, unless we can make torches do."

"I don't want no Sunbeamers prowling around my camp," her father declared petulantly. "I won't have it, neither." But he stood there passive while they dismounted. "The Sunbeam has done about all the damage it needs to do. I ain't goin' to stand for no more monkey business now, I can tell yuh that!"

On the ground, Vida turned her back upon him as if he were not there. "He's over here. You can bring a couple of
89

torches and see for yourselves," she told the boys, while her father was still speaking. "I told Poppy not to move him— we just covered him up, is all. We sent Pete out for the sheriff, you know—and the coroner. Pete is one of the herders. So be careful about your own tracks until we get a light. You can see from one side, I think—over here on these rocks."

Unconsciously she was taking the lead, as if she'd been in the habit of asserting her superior intelligence in every emergency; but her voice was strained and harsh with the repression she had put upon herself. Spider picked a blazing sage branch from the fire and moved up alongside her.

"You needn't come," he said gruffly. "You better stay back here by the fire."

"No, I'm going to see the thing through," she told him. "I've got to. I stand for our side; and you—no matter how you feel personally, you stand for the other."

Yet she stood back from the group when Spider stooped and pulled off the dirty square of canvas that covered the dead man. With face averted and eyes cast down, she saw only the rusty, run-down boots of her Uncle Jake, with the deep, hard creases which time and weather give to cheap footwear.

After a minute or two she looked up at the faces of the four bent forward as they stared in silence. The flicker of the torch flame upon their faces gave that weird Rembrandt effect of light and shadow which seems to waken the latent savagery in a man's eyes. Their brows were frowning, their breath sucked in at the horror they looked upon. Even Shelton's face showed a sternness never there before.

Then Spider bent lower, reached out a reluctant hand and with his finger tips felt the crushed bones in the neck. He lifted the dead man's arm and felt along the ribs while the two watched him. Then he stood up, drew in his breath sharply and backed away. Unexpectedly, it was Shelton who replaced the grimy canvas over the dead face. "Whereabouts are the tracks?" Spider asked the girl, in a low voice.

"Down here. I'll show you." She led the way around the great, flat outcropping of lava rock upon which her uncle must have been sitting when the murderer crept upon him. "Let me take the torch," she said, reaching back for it. "We'll have to keep out to one side, ourselves. He came up on these rocks, I guess. There isn't any mark until you get down in the bottom of the gully."

She led the way down the rocky bank, Shelton close behind her and the other three following. At the bottom she passed the smoldering brand slowly above the ground, hesitated while she looked back up the bank to verify the direction, and went forward again. Shelton caught her hand and pulled her back with a protective gesture.

"Let me go ahead. You don't know what you might be running into." He took the torch, whirled it around his head to fan the blaze and went forward.

He found it, and stopped abruptly, glancing back at the others. The three cowboys pressed close around him, staring down at a mark in the sand; the plain imprint of a boot pressed deep into the soft soil with the weight of the man who had walked there. Burney's boot, without the shadow of a doubt. And the toe was pointed up the bank toward where the dead man lay crumpled upon one side, with the bones of his neck crushed and his head twisted horribly upon his shoulder. A long stride down the gully—too long a stride for any of them to compass—lay another track which matched the first.

Without a word Spider reached and took the torch from Shelton's hand and led the way slowly down the gully. Other tracks he found; tracks leading away from the place, up toward the gloomy scars of the mountain a mile or so away.

Down the gully and across the wider swale, and part way up the farther hill they went, following those huge, betraying tracks. There the burning brand burned to charred embers, winking a sullen, red eye at them. They stopped and gave much time to the making of other torches, while Vida sat down on the steep slope and waited, a forlorn little figure dimly seen under the stars; a lonely little figure which made no response to Shelton's efforts to lighten her mood.

She sat with her elbows on her knees and her chin in her cupped palm, staring at the Great Dipper wheeling in its slow march around the North Star. Behind her a week-old moon slid out from behind a cloud bank where it had been hiding, and stood a moment upon the highest peak of the mountain, before it dropped down into the shadow world beyond. Out somewhere in that direction a coyote yapped and in the camp across the ridge the sheep dog barked shrill answer to the challenge.

In the brief moonlight, Vida lifted her head, thinking the boys had succeeded in lighting the torches. She turned, looked up the long slope silvered briefly by the moon, gave a start and sprang suddenly to her feet. "Oh, look! There he is— right up there on the hill, looking down at us!"

Spider dropped the match he had been nursing between his palms, gave one look and started running up the hill. The rest followed, with no clear knowledge of what it was all about. But for an instant Spider had seen a huge, dark figure outlined against the crescent moon.

At his first movement—or perhaps it was Vida's cry that did it—the figure disappeared. But Spider ran on, his hand on his six-shooter in its holster at his side. Behind him ran Spooky and Shelton and Breed Jim, with Vida climbing excitedly, close to Spider.

When they finally reached the top and stood looking down into the deep shadows of the rugged cañon beyond, where the moon could not send a single faint ray, but only made the shadows blacker in contrast to the lightened hilltop, they knew there was nothing more to be done. For the murderer, running downhill with those enormous strides of which he was capable, while they were panting up to where they had glimpsed him, could easily be a quarter of a mile from there by the time they arrived at the top. As hopeless as a dozen miles, so far as overtaking him was concerned.

CHAPTER EIGHTEEN

"IT WAS HORRIBLE!"

THEY RETURNED to camp, stopping frequently to peer behind them; with some nervousness, if the truth were known. Burney a murderer meant Burney a madman, and there is no guessing what wild notion a homicidal maniac may take.

The Sunbeam cowboys offered to relieve Williams from his mournful vigil and were repulsed with such finality that they could not well insist. Williams would not trust a Sun-beamer to watch over a dead dog, he declared. So Shelton and Spider escorted the girl to her camp wagon and left her there, while Spooky and Breed Jim rode back to the Sun-beam.

"I don't think we ought to leave Vida alone here," Shelton said uneasily, when they were riding away from the wagon. "If it's Burney, he's crazy, and he may do any horrible thing that comes into his mind. And she threatened him, remember. The last thing he said to us was about Vida accusing him of killing sheep. He may have done this just to get even, don't you think? And here is where—"

"Aw, keep your shirt on, Shep," Spider advised him petu-lantly. "What d' yuh think I am? I been aiming to stick around close till morning, anyway. If he shows up here, it'll be a case of shoot first and argue afterwards. You can't reason with a crazy man."

"You do believe it's Burney, then," Shelton observed, in a relieved tone. He had been prepared to argue the point. "I know it doesn't seem possible, but—"

"Maybe it ain't possible," Spider retorted glumly, "but there's the dead man—the way he was killed. That's a damn strong argument, if you ask me, Shep. And them tracks in the gully right down behind him. Them was Burney's tracks, just as sure as hell."

"Oh, say! Those tracks won't be there in the morning, you know," Shelton explained impulsively. "Spooky scraped them all out with his foot as he went past, just as you scraped out those alleged bear tracks over there where we found old Dutch."

"Hunh!" grunted Spider. " 'Bout what I'd 'a' done, if it was anything less than a murder. I done it over in the cañon, yes. There wasn't nothin' more'n some dead sheep against him then." He pulled up beside a low rock outcropping.

"This is far enough off, Shep. Hope yuh got plenty of smokin'—she's goin' to be a damn long night, if yuh ask me."

Shelton considered it a very good location and said so. They had stopped in plain sight of the white-topped wagon, and yet were far enough away to relieve the girl of any hu-miliating sense of being watched.

"All the same," Spider began where he had left off, "I could swear that was Burney I seen up on top of that hill, lookin' down at us in the gully."

"But if he went to Pocatello, as he said he was going to do, could he get back here so soon?" Shelton eased his long legs down into a sandy depression where the wind had gouged the soil away from the ledge.

"If he went to Pocatello," Spider repeated musingly. "I kinda think he did go. And if he did, he sure as hell turned right around and come back again. You seen his tracks, Shep. And a man can't leave his tracks where he ain't been, can he?"

He snuggled down against the smooth rock and bowed his head down behind Shelton's back, so that he could light his cigarette without letting the match blaze be seen.

"Everything points to Burney," he went on gloomily, after he had smoked for a time in silence, shading the cigarette with his gloved hand. "I believe it was him done it, all right. At the same time—" He paused while he settled his hat more firmly upon his head. "At the same time, I've got a sneaking notion he didn't. There's things that don't line up. It don't look right to me."

"What doesn't, Spider?"

"Well, unless you lied, or was crazy in the head, there's things that Burney don't fit into. Contradictions, you'd call 'em."

"I know it," Shelton conceded soberly. "He doesn't fit into any of it, as I see it, except those tracks. And it has occurred to me," he added, leaning closer to Spider, "you or I or anybody could put on a pair of Burney's boots and make big tracks. It would be a clever way of hiding our own tracks. And if those Williams men had an enemy who wanted to get vengeance on them or something, it would be a pretty smooth way of shifting suspicion, wouldn't it?"

"Yeah, it would, if he could take as long steps as Burney," Spider assented dryly. "*You* couldn't step in them tracks back there, Shep, and you're longer in the legs than the average man is."

"Well, but a tall man might step—"

A scream—the high, shrill scream of stark terror—brought

94

them both to their feet, their hearts thumping wildly. Without going for their horses, they ran leaping through the sage and rocks. Shelton stumbled over a root and nearly went down.

Without knowing why he did so, he shouted. And as he recovered his balance, a great, dark form left the wagon and went tearing off toward the distant ridge. Over where the sheep lay bedded down on the flat, the dogs barked and barked, with rumbling growls spacing the shrill staccato of their clamor.

Shelton's long legs overreached Spider's stride, carried him ahead so that he reached the wagon first, out of breath and weak with fear for the girl.

"Vida!" he gasped, clutching a wheel and clawing for the opening. "Vida! Are you all right?"

From over his head she answered him, pushing open the narrow door in the canvas wagon top. "Oh, I—oh, Shelton! He—came!"

She crouched in the doorway, one hand going out to touch his shoulder for comfort. "How did you get here so soon?" she asked bewilderedly, the shock of her experience still upon her.

"Why, we didn't go. Only over to those rocks, there. We—"

Spider came up panting. "You stay here, Shep, in case he doubles back. If he comes, *shoot*. And shoot quick." And he was gone, running in the direction the huge figure had taken.

"Oh, he mustn't go! Burney'll kill him!" gasped Vida, all her courage and her sturdy independence frightened out of her. She clung to Shelton, shivering with a nervous chill.

"He'll never get a sight of Burney," Shelton said shrewdly. "What did he do, Vida?"

She shivered again. "I was trying to get to sleep and I just couldn't, somehow. The whole thing—it haunts me. And then I thought I heard something outside and I lay there on the bed listening. And I was so scared I didn't seem able to move, not even to reach for my gun.

"And then this door was pushed open—and I screamed, I guess—I sort of heard myself yelling. But he couldn't get through it like any one else. It isn't so very wide, you see, and he's so big! He blocked the whole doorway. And then you hollered, and he backed out and I heard him running."

95

Spider had come up and was standing leaning against the wheel, his eyes searching the darkness. "He ain't anywhere within gunshot of here," he declared. "Could you tell which way he went?"

"Oh, I don't know—it was so horrible! He—might have killed me, like he did Uncle Jake!"

"He's crazy," Spider muttered fiercely. "Burney wouldn't hurt a muskeeter; not if he was in his right mind." His voice was low, saddened by the catastrophe which had overwhelmed his boss. "I've heard tell, Miss Williams that, the kinder and gentler a person is, the worse they act when they go crazy."

"That doesn't help any," she retorted sharply. "It doesn't make him a bit less horrible. Oh, I wish you could find him and kill him! We're none of us safe a minute while he's running loose."

She broke down then, completely. She sat crouching just inside the narrow doorway and sobbed hysterically, her arms folded upon the doorsill. Perched outside, Shelton tried to calm her with a diffident pat now and then on her heaving shoulders.

Spider wandered away again, in the vain hope of getting some clue to Burney's whereabouts. He had an uneasy feeling that the maniac might linger in their vicinity, watching for a chance to rush in and complete the diabolical deed his insane brain had planned. Sane, Burney did not easily change his plans, but forged doggedly ahead, ignoring all obstacles. It seemed as though his sick brain might still follow that habit.

In that faint light which the stars gave, it was too dark to see anything clearly. From where he walked in the sage, the rock outcropping was a vague blot against the horizon. The dogs were still barking intermittently, but their yapping now seemed to be directed chiefly at their charges, forcing stray animals back into the huddled band.

He returned again to the wagon and found that Vida was still crying in a subdued, tired way that went straight to the big soft heart of Spider. In the dim light he looked inquiringly at Shelton who sat there speechless, as if he felt his helplessness in the face of a mood like hers. Spider moved closer and laid a hand timidly upon Vida's bowed shoulder.

96

"You don't want to feel so bad about it," he said bashfully. "A man's got to go when his time's called, and if this hadn't been your Uncle Jake's time, it never woulda happened. And as for you—why, I reckon we'll take mighty good care you don't get hurt. Anyway, we'll round Burney up tomorrow. He can't get away. He's so ungodly big he can't beat it outa the country and hide anywheres in town, no more than a elephant could hide in a cabbage patch. And if he stays in these hills, we're bound to get him."

He spoke with the authority of a range man and his words carried weight. Vida lifted her head from her arms and wiped her eyes.

"I know it," she assented apologetically. "I'm not a coward, ordinarily. I believe I could really kill him myself, if I met him in daylight. I—I guess it was just a case of nerves. I don't cry very often. If I cried every time I felt badly," she said impatiently, "I wouldn't have time for anything else. But —I did get an awful scare."

"Lordy, it was enough to scare any one," Shelton hastened to assure her.

"Well, I thought I was alone, except for the herder over there with his sheep, and I knew he never would hear anything or have the nerve to come over here and see what was wrong, if he did hear. He bedded the sheep down away over there on the flat, where nothing can sneak up on the band. So I—I just felt that was the end of me, when Burney came trying to push in through the door."

"That was my fault, I reckon," Spider said uncomfortably. "We'd oughta told you we was goin' to hang around close."

"Well, you're so awfully independent, I was afraid you wouldn't like it if you knew we were close by," Shelton confessed.

"Well, I like it now, all right," Vida gave a little laugh. "I'll scream again if you move away from this wagon."

Whereupon the two disposed themselves as comfortably as possible on the ground and smoked and talked and waited for the sun.

CHAPTER NINETEEN

THEY GO AFTER BURNEY

T HE APPETIZING odor of bacon and coffee drifted out into the dawn. The white wagon top glowed rosily as the East blushed with royal purples and crimsons, but the three gave it not a glance. The two men ate hungrily, well aware of the hard day ahead, and set forth upon the man trail; grimly, determined to go on until they found the murderer; ready to kill if they came face to face with him. Spider had armed himself with an old shotgun which Vida lent him, besides his forty-five. Shelton had only his revolver; and Vida, who went along for the simple reason that she was afraid not to go, had her six-shooter and the little twenty-two that seemed so ridiculously inadequate in a fight.

Tracks they found, almost immediately; the great, telltale footprints spaced far apart in the stride only possible to a giant like Burney. Spider's eyes clouded anew when he discovered them in the sandy soil, for he had liked Burney well. They had eaten at the same table, slept under the same tent, and had used tobacco from the same sack with that democratic freedom which is the true essence of the Western type. He had watched over Burney's cattle; with Burney's money he had paid for the clothes which he wore. He had been proud of Burney's huge frame, of his tremendous strength, of his fairness, and of the quiet masterfulness of his manner.

Big in every way he had believed Burney to be. Too big, certainly, for petty crime or wanton murder; so big that he did not need to defend himself or his rights with the weapons of ordinary men. In the two or three years that Spider had known him, Burney never had owned or carried a gun. He never hunted animals, either for pleasure or profit—and for men he did not need a weapon. That was why he killed now with his hands.

The trail wound here and there through the sage and there were times when they lost it altogether. But the general trend of the tracks was toward the highest, roughest peak of the hills, so that Spider, heading for the most logical route into its deep-scarred cañons, picked up the trail twice after several minutes of traveling by guess over rocky ground.

Just behind him walked Vida, with Shelton bringing up the rear. The girl's face was drawn and colorless from worry and lack of sleep and food; for the breakfast which she had cooked for the two men she herself had left untouched, except for a few sips of black coffee. Since they must travel rough country where a horse would be useless, the three had set out afoot, leaving their horses picketed near the wagon. She seemed tireless, yet the two tried to save her strength for her, since she seemed to have no care for herself. But she would not have it so. If they sat down to rest after a sharp climb, Vida went on ahead—which gave Shelton and Spider some anxious moments and sent them hurrying after her. Once, Spider remonstrated with her for taking unnecessary risks, but she answered him sharply.

"When I hear a rattler," she said, "I never quit till I find him and kill him. That's because I'm scared of snakes. And I'm so scared of that great big beast of a Burney that I won't take a long breath until I catch him. So long as he's free and I don't know where he is, I'm—I just expect every minute he'll sneak up and grab me."

"Not while we're here, he won't," Shelton exclaimed, repressing a shiver of horror at the thought. "You mustn't go ahead like that, Vida. Stay back with us."

"Yeah," Spider added, "and you've got to save yourself, too. We're a long ways from camp a'ready. I wisht now we'd brought the horses."

"You don't neither," she contradicted him flatly. "You knew he'd take to the hills where we couldn't ride. He's afoot, and he'd be sure to pick the roughest going he could find. And it looks to me as if we're up against it right now. He's got us stopped, if you want my opinion."

This, because they had come to a stand before a bare cliff which shut off the small box cañon they had entered at its mouth, encouraged by two of the huge boot tracks they were following. These they had found in the loose sand of a dry channel leading up the cañon. And while there were no more, they had been certain they were on the right trail. The cañon walls had been high and precipitous, with overhanging ledges

99

of rock unbroken save where slides had ripped off great sections here and there and left spaces unclimbable because of the banks of shale.

The hills were full of such cañons, and frequently they were passable at the head, giving access either to a higher plateau or to other cañons leading on into the hills. Here, however, the cañon head was blocked with a cliff running straight across.

"Maybe Burney could get up there," Spider said dubiously, eyeing the narrow ledge two feet above his highest reach. "You try it, Shep."

Whereupon Shelton stood beneath the ledge and jumped, trying to hook his fingers over the top. He tried three times and failed to get a hold to help him pull himself up.

"No go," he panted, after the third futile attempt. "I could climb up on your shoulders and get up that way, Spider. But what would be the use? Burney didn't have any one to boost him up, so I don't believe he went this way at all."

"Well, unless there's some other way outa here, we're done for the present," Spider disgustedly agreed.

Nevertheless, they searched the cliff from wall to wall. They stood back and stared at the ledge, debating with each other whether it would be possible for a man as big as Burney to climb up there. Shelton was the last to give up, but even he consented at last to go back, at least as far as the cañon's mouth. "Maybe we could follow the top of the cañon around to the head of it up here and pick up the trail where he climbed out," Spider suggested.

So they went back down the cañon, climbed laboriously up the bluff which became its right wall farther along, and went on. The way was rough; so rough that Spider began to feel more and more uneasy on account of the girl. But until they reached the point where they could look down the cliff that had halted them in the cañon below, she remained deaf to his arguments or to Shelton's pleas.

Then, gazing out over the wild expanse, she saw how fruitless the search was going to be. Like the black cañon they had reached the night before, they looked upon a thousand hiding places, any one of which would be impregnable, so far as they were concerned. It was a fact that Burney might be an impassable mile or two away, absolutely safe from their most eager pursuit, or he might be hiding almost within reach of his long arm from them.

Certainly there was no use in going farther. With their backs to a cliff that made them safe from the rear, they rested awhile, and then made their way dispiritedly down to where the land rolled gently out to the arid plains where the Williams sheep had foraged among the sage for the grass which the winter snows and spring rains had coaxed into growing there.

When they could look down over the slopes to where the dead man still lay under his canvas covering, Spider's sharp eyes saw movement there of various black objects which he knew to be men and horses. They might be fellows whom Spooky and Jim had brought over, or it might easily be the coroner whom Vida had said one of their herders had gone after. Whoever it was, the three wanted to know what was going on, and they hurried down the long, sloping ridge that would bring them the quickest to the camp.

As they trudged wearily up to the gruesome spot, they recognized Spooky and Jim amongst the group. Spider recognized others also: Bell, the sheriff, and also the coroner, whose name was Walters. And there were men whom the coroner had probably brought with him to make up a jury. Spider knew most of them, having lived in that country for more than two years.

Over behind the group, half sitting against the ledge, was one at sight of whom Vida gave a suppressed scream and dodged in behind Spider. "Oh, they got him!" she cried.

At the sound of her voice, Burney stood up; huge, quiescent, towering above the others with the patient inaction of a great Newfoundland dog in the midst of a pack of terriers. He was not handcuffed nor was he under any apparent restraint, which caused Spider to reach for his gun just as a precautionary measure.

For all her valiant attitude during the day in the hills, Vida hung back, afraid to face the situation. But with Spider and Shelton between Burney and herself, she reluctantly approached the group, sidling in close beside her father.

Spider went straight up to the sheriff, a broad-shouldered, red-faced man with a neck like a bull, who stood a little to one side filling a blackened old pipe. His air of indifference, standing there with his back toward Burney, made Spider swear under his breath. The sheriff glanced up at him from under his black hat brim, nodded a greeting with a quizzical twist of his lips and turned so that he could glance sidelong toward the giant.

Spider looked that way also. "Where did you get Burney?" he asked in an undertone. And he added, "I s'pose you know your business—you been workin' at it long enough—but I should think you'd want to chain him up, instead of leaving him loose like that."

The sheriff made two attempts to light a match on his lifted leg, got it going at last and cupped the flame with his two hands over the pipe bowl.

"I didn't git 'im," he drawled, when he had the pipe going to his satisfaction. "Burney got me. The fellow Williams sent in caught the night train to Pocatello—I was down there on business. He was huntin' around town for me and Burney happened to hear about it. So he come and told me there'd been a murder, up this way, and I was wanted. He went along with me and we got the particulars from the man. So then Burney, he come on up with us.

"Seems like Williams accuses Burney of doin' the killing, but that's all poppycock, in my opinion." He jerked his head backward toward the coroner, who was down on one knee examining the corpse. "It's up to him," he said. "He'll likely be able to place the time of the murder, but if it was yesterday, as Williams claims it was, Burney's got a gilt-edged alibi. He was in Pocatello all day yesterday."

"You sure uh that?" Spider plucked Bell by the arm and drew him farther away. "Last night," he stated deliberately, "Burney came to the wagon where Miss Williams was and tried to git in. She saw him at the door and screamed, and me and that young feller over there heard her and ran up. Burney beat it when he heard us coming—"

Bell had been shaking his beefy head throughout the speech, wordlessly denying every bit of it. Now, he began to tap Spider impressively on the chest with his forefinger.

"Now you listen to me, young feller," he rumbled. "Burney was with me last night in Pocatello. We made a round of the saloons and the red lights, lookin' for a feller I had a warrant for. We caught the early train to Corona together. He ain't been out uh my sight all day. So it wasn't him you seen last night."

"But there was his tracks to prove it was him," Spider insisted. "After workin' at the Sunbeam long as I have, I couldn't hardly make a mistake in the boss's track; not when they're big as Burney's. We tracked him up into the hills. And earlier in the evening, I seen him myself for a minute, standin' over there right on that ridge."

"Oh, hell!" exclaimed the sheriff impatiently. "You seen what wasn't there, then. Ain't I just been telling you Alec Burney was with me from nine o'clock till now?" He put his pipe back into his mouth, sucked hard on it for a few breaths, and grinned wryly with a humorous puckering of his lips.

"They tell me you got a spook out here in these hills, Spider," he drawled. "Mebbe that's what you seen. You sure as hell didn't see Alec Burney. There's a dozen men—yes, a hundred!—that can swear to that. Everybody's gawked at him, every place we went. He ain't," he said dryly, "a man that's easy mistook."

"No, you're right. He ain't," Spider agreed, and went away and sat down upon a rock, and rested his elbows on his spread knees and stared hard at the ground. He wanted to think this thing out, yet he was too bewildered to think. As he had told Shelton before, not one single, solitary fact seemed to fit in with any other fact.

"The things you know for a fact are every one of 'em plumb impossible," he muttered to himself, while he made himself a smoke. He glanced up at the stark, frowning hills above them. "I guess mebbe it must be spooks," he thought. And that was as far toward a solution of the mystery as Spider seemed able to go.

CHAPTER TWENTY

"BURNEY WAS IN POCATELLO"

V IDA sidled around Burney at a distance of two rods and so came up to Spider. She was shaking with nervousness and she was white and full of indignation. Shelton, as may be supposed, followed close behind her, his sunken eyes looking almost black with excitement and his handsome face eloquent of his mental disturbance.

"What's that sheriff thinking of?" Vida demanded resentfully. "Why are they letting Burney walk around free like that? Poppy says he isn't even under arrest."

Spider lifted his head and looked gloomily at the two. "I know he ain't. This thing's all balled up and there don't nobody know where they're at. Burney come up from Pocatello this morning with the sheriff. He was there yesterday and all last night. The sheriff says Burney hunted him up and told him your herder wanted to see him, and come along with him."

"But how *could* he? He was trying to get in our wagon last night. I'd swear to that before any jury in the land. How could he be in Pocatello when he was here?"

"Search me," said Spider glumly.

"Well, what are they all fooling around about, now?" Shelton smoothed the gravel off a flat bowlder so that Vida could sit down. "Why don't they do something?" he asked, in what came near to being a truculent tone.

"Oh, they're getting ready for the inquest, I guess. That's the coroner monkeying around the body, now. And all them other fellows are the jury. You and me and Vida and her dad and the herder will all have to testify, I reckon. Mebbe they'll want Spooky and Jim too." The mystery was still weighing heavily on Spider's mind and his tone was apathetic. No inquest was going to explain how Burney could be in two places at once, he was thinking.

"Well, I wish to goodness they'd get busy," Vida said peevishly and glared at the group as if they all were her enemies. "I'll break loose and scream if somebody doesn't do something pretty quick. It's all like a nightmare to me. I just can't make myself believe that's Uncle Jake lying there under that tarp—"

"Don't try to believe it," Shelton advised her, with a flash of his shrewd intelligence. "Just slide through all this as easily as you can. It isn't a thing that one should be expected to believe. I don't, myself, when you come right down to it. I can't believe that Burney would stand there like that, with his hands in his pockets, just as if he were a—a mere by-stander."

"He's the murderer. He must be. No one else could possibly have done it," Vida pointed out insistently.

The coroner rose up from where he had been kneeling, beckoned to the sheriff and the two conferred interminably, it seemed to those three sitting apart. Yet in a very few minutes it was ended and the coroner was choosing his jury, which included all of the strangers standing around. He was a pudgy little man, yet when he took off his hat—whether in deference to the dead, the duty vested in him or to the one lady present, Shelton could not determine—and when he cleared his throat and began to speak, a grim dignity invested his presence and his words.

Vida drew a long breath and straightened her shoulders, for the first time comforted and reassured by the presence of the law. The intangible weight of responsibility that had felt so like a real burden upon her shoulders, lifted. The sheriff and the coroner and all those men—they would deal with Alec Burney as he deserved. Though he stood free, a little apart from the others, with his pipe in his mouth and one hand in his gray coat pocket, he still was within the grip of the law. The sheriff must be watching him like a hawk, even though he did act as if Burney was farthest from his mind. He might act careless, but he wouldn't let Burney get away. He'd shoot him first.

And then, as the inquest proceeded and her father testified, and Pete and Spooky and Spider and Jim, Vida began to feel a vague discomfort. The jury went solemnly down into the little gully to look at the tracks and she could imagine how Burney would look when they came back and told what they had found.

The jury filed back up the bank, sweating from the exertion. They looked questioning at Vida's father, who had sworn that Burney's tracks were in that gully and they looked at the herder Pete, who had testified to the same thing (Spooky, Spider and Breed Jim had been less definite in their statements).

"Your honor, we couldn't find any tracks like them the two witnesses described," the spokesman declared rather querulously. "Bell, here, can swear to that."

"Did you look where they said to look?" the coroner demanded solemnly.

"Yes, we did. We looked all over. There's been a lot of trackin' back and forth, but all the tracks we saw—and I guess we saw all there is—ain't any different from anybody's tracks. There are no tracks that Mr. Burney could of made, your honor."

Vida could not understand that. She half started to rise, but Spider shook his head at her and she sank back again. Her eyes were wide open, blazing with indignation, but Spider met them with a calm she could not ignore.

"They'll call yuh when they want yuh," he whispered behind his hand.

"But those tracks *are* there. You know they are. You both saw them!"

"Well, we ain't runnin' this inquest. Listen to the rest. They'd throw us in the cooler if we got up now and butted in on the proceedin's," Spider quelled her rebellion.

So Vida sat still and listened. The sheriff was being sworn, just like any common man. She was more or less prepared for his testimony, yet it sounded terribly final and unassailable now when he made the statements under oath. He told just what time of day it was yesterday when he first saw Alec Burney on the street in Pocatello. Burney was coming out of the bank, and they stood and talked for a few minutes. That was about half-past two. Then he saw Burney in a restaurant at six, though he did not speak to him at that time. And at about nine o'clock that evening, he again met Burney, who joined him in looking for a man the sheriff had orders to pick up on a robbery charge in Salt Lake, and also because a warrant had been sworn out against him for a fight he had got into in the depot waiting room. By the time the sheriff was through, no one could possibly believe that Burney had been here, murdering her uncle Jake.

Her father was recalled and told of the sheep that had been killed, and of Burney's visit to camp on the morning when he had ordered Williams off the range with his sheep. He proved a possible motive for the crime, but that did not offset the sheriff's amazing evidence or the mystery of the tracks that had disappeared.

There was a minute or two of whispered consultation and a question which the foreman asked the coroner concerning the manner of death.

"I find," replied the coroner, "that the deceased undoubtedly came to his death by having his neck broken by twisting. Four ribs are also broken, evidently by crushing. There are no bullet wounds, nor any other marks of violence, except some scratches on the scalp, behind the ear. These, I judge, were made by finger nails, in gripping the head to twist it."

Vida shivered. And then came the most amazing thing of all, in her opinion. The jury whispered for a while and the foreman gave their verdict. And the verdict was that her Uncle Jake had met his death at the hands of some person unknown to them—with Alec Burney standing there within twenty feet of them, his great, murderous hands hidden in his pockets!

She sprang to her feet to denounce them all as cowards and fools and liars. But when she stood up and had gotten as far as, "Oh, you—" everything went black and the entire scene was blotted out of existence so far as she was concerned.

When she came to herself again, she was on a bed in the sheep wagon, with a wet towel wadded on her forehead, trickling water down her neck. Her father was scorching the bacon outside and the coroner was talking to him about free wool and explaining why it would be a disaster for the entire country, from Maine to California.

Vida lay there, trying to piece things together; trying also to muster enough energy to call out to Poppy that he'd better let free wool alone and attend to the bacon. But neither seemed worth the effort, so presently she went to sleep.

When she woke again, it was night and a cool wind was

stirring the sage and flapping a loose bit of canvas in the doorway. She did not know where her father was, but she supposed he was asleep under the wagon, where he always made up his bed when they were together. It occurred to her to be thankful that Uncle Jake had been a very neat house-keeper who never permitted any rancid odors of stale cooking in his wagon. She liked the cool, sweet smell of the sage that drifted in to her through the little, open window over the bed.

She wondered if they had buried Uncle Jake; or would they have the funeral to-morrow? Not much of a funeral, she was afraid, with no coffin and no preacher or anything. Maybe they had carried him away to town, though that did not seem likely, either. They would have to use the sheep wagon —and they wouldn't do that, while she was asleep inside. Furthermore, she could tell by the sage smell outside that they were in the high country. Corona squatted down in a hot little flat, all adobe and lava rock. There wasn't enough sage to smell within a mile of the place.

How could Burney be in Pocatello and away out here at the same time? How could he make tracks where he hadn't been? Maybe Piute Hills were really haunted, after all. It did seem queer that all the boys at the Sunbeam would make up a story about a ghost and stick to it the way they had done. Or maybe it was a great, enormous grizzly, just as Shelton believed—when he wasn't believing it was Burney or a ghost. But if it were a bear—

She fell asleep again and dreamed that she was tracking Burney up a long cañon, and that the tracks came and went in the sand before her eyes without any human aid or explanation. Then she dreamed that she was in a blind cañon with no way out except through the mouth where she had entered, and a grizzly bear ten feet high came walking down toward her on his hind legs, grinning and showing all his teeth, and saying in a deep voice, "Some one's been eating my soup!"

But her dream shifted, as dreams have a fashion of doing. It was Burney, and he was looking for her, and she was hiding in there, trying to scrooch down behind a rock no bigger than her head. She saw him creeping up the cañon, a gigantic figure in the deep shadows of the high walls. And suddenly the rock began to shrink smaller and smaller until it was only a pebble and there was no place to hide.

Burney was coming closer and closer, peering this way and that, with his little, deep-set, twinkling eyes. Oddly enough, he had both hands stuffed deep in his pockets. He had not yet discovered her where she cowered against the bare wall of the cañon, but he would see her presently. He was so close that she could hear his footsteps crunching—

The wagon tilted six inches, heaved upward from below, and Vida awoke with a start. She found herself sitting up on the hard bunk, and her heart was not beating at all; then it gave a heavy flop at the base of her neck. She screamed without any conscious volition; a shriek of terror.

Again the wagon heaved upward, so that she must cling to the boarded edge of the bunk. It felt as if men were prying it out of a mudhole with a long pole under the axle. Like a rabbit scared out of its hiding place, she darted suddenly away from the bed and down the lurching length of the wagon box to the narrow doorway, jerked the door open and looked out.

She knew then what it was she feared. And she knew that she was afraid for her father, whose bed was always made up under the wagon and who slept heavily, as tired, slow-thinking men do sleep, when their lives are spent in the open. Suddenly the wagon settled down on its four wheels. There was a scurrying rush of some huge creature. It was behind the wagon, where Vida could not see. She felt for her rifle, but it was not there in the corner by the door where she always kept it. And then she remembered that this was not their wagon, but Uncle Jake's. "Poppy!" she called out in terror again. *"Poppy!* where are you?"

Out somewhere in the dark, above the whispering of the wind in the sage, a hoarse scream answered her. Human—and yet not human. Mocking, maniacal, horrible. It was the most awful sound that Vida had ever heard in her life; a squall, a cry—something she could find no name to describe.

Her memory flew back to the tales of ghosts and demons that an old Scotch woman had told her years ago. Warlock—that was it. A warlock, such as Maggie McDonald had told about, that haunted the heath behind the village, where

109

strange deaths occurred periodically in the dark of the moon. Men and women who were found strangled, none knew how or why.

CHAPTER TWENTY-ONE

A BULLET WILL GET HIM

Back in the shadows where the moon could not betray her to the devil that roamed without, Vida crouched down in the wagon box, half fainting with fright. She had laughed at those old tales of warlock, except when she shivered during the actual telling. But now, to-night, the thing seemed real and imminently menacing. She felt its uncanny presence bounding away over the sage, taking whatever shape it fancied, leaving what trail it would for men to puzzle over.

She hid her face in her circling arms and shivered. Now she saw why it was that Burney had seemed to be in two places at once; why it was that Shelton and Spider and Spooky had felt some eerie thing following them at night. They might have been killed. No one was safe from a warlock. No one.

She could not have spent more than a minute or two crouching there in the grip of superstitious fear, but it seemed to her that she must have cowered in that corner against the grub box for at least an hour. Then she lifted her head and listened. It was not imagination. She heard a stir beneath the wagon, a sound between a grunt and a groan.

"Poppy!" she cried out, getting unsteadily to her feet. "What was it, Poppy? Are you hurt?"

The sound of her own voice steadied her, snapped her back into her old, efficient self. She felt her way back to the rear of the wagon. In the dim light of the moon shining faintly on the canvas, she groped with her fingers along a rough shelf over the bed where she thought her father might have put her revolver.

Her hand struck against the cool barrel. She caught it up eagerly and went hurrying back to the door, which was still open and swung slowly back and forth in the breeze, like the pendulum of a clock almost run down for lack of winding. She climbed down over the front of the wagon box (any one at all familiar with sheep wagons will know that they are not very conveniently arranged for getting in and out) and crept between the front wheels, where her father always put the head of his bed.

It was dark there and the moon had set a black shadow of the wagon top down upon the eastern side. Vida groped with one hand—the other held her revolver. "Poppy! Why don't you answer me? Where are you?" she cried sharply.

The vague outline of his squat figure detached itself from the shadow of the wagon and he stood plainly revealed in the moonlight.

"If I could git a sight of 'im, I'd shoot him down like I would a coyote," he snarled. "Where be yuh, Vida? Tore m' shirt half off'm me, trying to git his hands on m' throat! All that saved me was the bigness of 'im. He got hung up between the wagon wheels, and he didn't know just how I was layin'. If I'd 'a' had my head out in the open, he'd 'a' killed me, sure.

"Man like that had oughta be hung up by the heels over a slow fire! Killin's too good for a feller like that. Did yuh hear him holler, Vida? Tried to sound like a mountain lion— thought he'd fool somebuddy, mebbe. But it didn't work worth a cent. He can't fool *me!* I seen 'im in the moonlight when he turned tail to run. I seen 'im plain as day."

"And was it Burney?" Vida had crawled back from under the wagon, and the two stood together just within the shadow, staring off into the moonlit, whispering sage which the breeze moved so that it seemed alive.

"A course it was Burney! He needn't to think he c'n fool *me!* He backed out into the moonlight for a minute, and I seen him, plainer'n what I see you. A course it was Burney!

"He's a cute one—pertendin' to be in Pocatello, and at home and every damn place, except where he's at. But he can't fool *me.* He's cute, but he ain't cute enough. He crawled out and stood up in the moonlight. If I'd 'a' had m' gun in m' hands right then, I sure would uh fixed him! Tried to murder me in m' sleep! He would 'a', too, if he hadn't uh been so all-fired big he couldn't get under the wagon."

Away off on the flat, where the sheep were bedded down

111

in the care of a herder, a dog began to bark hysterically with the sharp staccato of alarm; yelped once and was still. A few mother sheep blatted as if they were frightened, and the herder yelled some shrill command; yelled just once and did not yell again.

Vida shuddered. "I'll bet he went over there, amongst the sheep," she whispered. Then she took a fresh grip on her courage and started to run toward the disturbance. She had forgotten all about her conviction that a warlock was abroad, working his will upon defenseless humans. Her father had said that it was Burney, and big as he was, Vida did not fear him, so long as she had a gun in her hand.

"Come on, Poppy!" she called over her shoulder at her father, who still hesitated and grumbled threats in the shadow of the wagon. "Come on and help me get him! He isn't so big that a bullet won't stop him—come on!"

"You come on back here!" cried her father, with his voice raised in futile command while he stayed where he was. "Come on back! You can't do nothin' in the dark!"

"He may be killing Walt Smith!" Vida flung the sentence back at him and ran the faster. But her father remained by the wagon and shouted commands and imprecations after her as she ran.

She topped the last low ridge that marked the edge of the sage-covered flat where the sheep had been held for safety, and stood still for a minute, trying to see what was taking place out there where the band was huddled.

The moon silvered the plain with a soft light. She could see as far as Pillar Butte, a vague, dark blur against the star-sprinkled purple which was the sky. Then, quite suddenly, the moonlight darkened so that she could not see ten rods. She turned to see why and a streak of vivid yellow gashed the night like a flaming sword.

A thunderstorm, common enough in that country, was sweeping up from the southwest. Already it had swallowed the moon so deeply that Vida, staring upward, could see only a faint, white blur where it had disappeared. And while she stared with her face turned upward, she heard a cry down there before her on the flat. A man's cry for help. It was not so very far away, either. She swung instantly and faced that way, wishing for the lightning that would cut away the darkness.

"This way! Come this way!" she cried as loudly as she could, against the low mutter of the thunder, and with her thumb pulled back the hammer of her gun.

It was Walt Smith, the tow-headed Mormon herder. He was running in great lunging strides. She could hear him rustling the sagebushes as he jumped over them or forged through a close-growing clump.

And then came the lightning again, slashing the clouds and making them look like a black velvet curtain swept aside to give a glimpse of the brilliance behind. The whole plain was lighted more clearly than by the moon. Standing there with the lightning behind her, she saw Walt Smith running toward her like a chased rabbit scurrying to its burrow. And behind him she saw the huge figure of a man, who came on with giant strides, leaping clean over what bushes were in his way.

Then the darkness dropped and made the night darker after the glare. She could see nothing. The heavy roll of thunder beat down whatever cry might have come from the herder. But the lightning flashed again and Walt was close; so close that she could see he had no hat on, and that his tow hair was bushy around his face, blowing in the wind as he ran. And that giant who came behind—he was close too. In a few more strides he would be upon Walt.

Almost mechanically Vida raised her six-shooter and fired straight at his middle. The big man swerved sharply aside and she fired again and again. She had no more feeling in the matter than if she were trying to hit a coyote that had been stealing lambs from the flock. It did not occur to her then that she was trying to take the life of a man.

She saw him whirl and start back the way he had come —and then black darkness shut down again. She could hear Walt Smith come puffing up the slope, breathing stertorously, with little, whimpering sounds as he ran. Vida stood waiting for him, her lip curled with contempt. What a rabbit he was! Running to a girl for protection! She should think he would be ashamed to come near her.

Walt had a gun. The herders carried rifles to shoot the

marauding coyotes that always skulked close to a band of sheep. Why didn't he shoot, instead of running like a scared jackrabbit? Burney would not have come after him if Walt had used his gun. She was beginning vaguely to understand that Burney was afraid of a gun. A bullet was the only thing more powerful, swifter and more dangerous than he was. He could not fight and overcome a bullet. He could not catch one on its singing flight and twist the neck of it and kill it. Burney was afraid of a gun. And once she realized the truth, Vida lost her last trace of fear.

So she felt strong and contemptuously competent as Walt came panting up to where she stood, and between great sobbing breaths told her how Burney had got among the sheep, and how a dog had run out at him, and Burney had killed the dog. He said that he had shouted for the other dog that was off chasing a coyote on the far side of the band, and that Burney had come at him, then, like a charging elephant.

"And you didn't have sense enough to shoot!" she made bitter comment, stepping back away from him: "You and Poppy make me tired. I'll bet you dropped your gun and started to run the minute you saw him coming."

"No, I never done anything of the sort!" Walt hastened to deny. "I kep' my gun in my hands. I got it now. But I never had no chance to use it. He—he was comin' *right at* me!"

CHAPTER TWENTY-TWO

"BURNEY WAS GONE LAST NIGHT"

IN THE FACE of the freshening wind, Vida made her way back to where her father stood guard over the empty sheep wagon and waited impatiently for her return. Behind her tagged Walt Smith, puffing and pasty white from the scare he had gotten.

"Poppy, either you or Walt will have to go and stay with the sheep," she announced firmly, when she came near and the lightning split the darkness, revealing him to her. "Burney killed one of the dogs just now, but you needn't be scared, either one of you. I just discovered he's deathly afraid of a gun. I know he never carries one; he depends on brute strength and cunning, I guess. But you should have seen him take to his heels as soon as I began shooting at him. If he shows up again, you're bound to see him with the lightning flashing this way. Just take a shot at him and he'll turn tail and head for the hills."

"He ought to be killed!" her father snarled ineffectively. "Tried to murder me to-night, right in my own bed. If he hadn't got hung up between the wagon wheels, I'd 'a' been killed in cold blood. Any man that'll sneak around in the dark murderin'—"

A disheartened look of unavailing anger darkened Vida's sensitive face. "You'll have the rest of your life to talk about that. Some one will have to get back to those sheep before they start drifting. You can suit yourselves which one of you goes. It's going to storm pretty quick, and storm hard too. I hope you men don't expect me to get out there and herd sheep all night. I'm about all in, right now. I'm going to get something to eat and rest until morning."

She started to climb up into the wagon, but stopped in the doorway and turned toward the two who stood there looking at her, silenced by her cold logic but reluctant to leave the camp.

She looked down at them impassively. "Where's the sheriff, Poppy?" she asked. "He didn't go off back to town, did he, without doing anything more about the murder? And what's he going to do about Burney?"

"I ain't runnin' the sheriff's business," her father retorted, with the querulousness of the weak-souled. "How should I know where he's at? Went off to town with the coroner, I guess, after we buried Jake.

"He couldn't do nothing about Burney; not after the coroner's jury give their verdict. A sheriff can't run a man in without a warrant," he explained, in that tone of weary tolerance of a woman's ignorance which some men love to assume. "Pete seen Burney in Pocatello, and the sheriff swore Burney was there all the time. That there constitutes a alibi. You got to *git* something on Burney before he can be arrested."

"Yes, and he'd run loose a good long while before *you*

115

ever did anything about it, except talk!" she cried bitterly. "And it was your own brother he killed. And your sheep. And you haven't done a thing about it from the very first, except mumble and complain and tell what ought to be done."

She whirled on the herder with a fierceness that drove him back a pace. "Walt Smith, you get back out there and look after those sheep! What do you think we're paying you for? You needn't be afraid of Burney—I'm not, any more. You saw me prove that all you have to do is shoot, and he'll run. You saw how he turned and headed the other way when I took a shot at him, didn't you? But you needn't worry; he's halfway home by this time."

She waited there in the doorway until she saw Walt turn reluctantly and go off toward the sheep. She upbraided her father then for his weakness that would waste precious minutes in useless clamor, when he might have dropped Burney in his tracks. In the morning, she declared, she meant to get out after Burney herself, seeing no one else in camp had the nerve to do it.

When she had made her feelings and her intentions perfectly clear to him—thereby calming and clarifying her own thoughts—she ate cold fried bacon laid between two slices of very good bread which she herself had baked, and finished with a dish of stewed, dried apples and a cup of cold coffee.

After that she lay down upon her hard bed with her six-shooter cuddled under her pillow, where her fingers could touch the cool butt of it, and listened to the grumbling mutter of the storm and watched the searing lightning flashing intermittent glares of light upon the bowed canvas roof.

She fell asleep so. For she was young and healthy and sturdy of spirit, and she had seen Burney, the giant, turn and run from her and her gun. Now that she had lost her fear of him, her nerves were steady and she slept like a child.

The rain came suddenly, pelting the sage land with great drops of cold water hurled to earth by the gale that blew from out the west. Sheets of water like a gray wall, with the slashing swordthrusts of lightning and the splitting crash of thunder—and still she slept. All her life she had known these terrific thunderstorms of the plains country, and the

116

shelter of that twelve-ounce canvas over her head spelled security to her nerves.

Her father pottered peevishly about, piling harness and saddles under the wagon and moving his blankets up under the canvas top. While he worked, he muttered querulously to himself all the things he would say to Burney if ever he met him face to face. When his sterile imagination would yield no more invective, he cursed the passionate fury of the storm and the vileness of a fate that placed him out in the desert with a bunch of sheep.

He did not think of the weary girl asleep in the bunk while he spread his bed upon the floor between the stove and the hinged table. Still mumbling to himself, he lay down at last for his belated rest. And through it all Vida slept quietly, heavily, utterly worn out and gathering strength for what was to come.

Morning brought Shelton and Spider galloping down from the ridge, anxious to know how she had fared and to learn whether they had seen or heard anything of her uncle's murderer. That, at least, was their professed errand, though Shelton probably had a stronger reason for riding that way so early in the morning.

Vida was washing dishes on a box beside the smoldering camp fire when they rode up. She was quite alone, since her father had gone out to take charge of the sheep, leaving Walt Smith to sleep as best he might with his blankets spread under a large sage-bush near his improvised camp.

Spider was somber-eyed and taciturn with the trouble that had come upon the Sunbeam. Shelton, once he saw Vida looking her natural self and apparently preoccupied with her domestic duties, beamed down upon her with the eager interest in life which she had come to associate with him.

"Well, you should stand up and make a bow and greet our new officer of the law," he cried gayly, wanting to see the smile that could transform her face so completely. "Our worthy sheriff swore Spider in as a deputy before he left yesterday. He said that he wanted Spider to feel that he had the full authority of the law behind him, in case any emergency arose or we discovered anything in the way of more evidence."

117

Vida's smile was faint. She gave Spider a curious look. "That means you've sworn to uphold the law," she observed shrewdly, "and not to show partiality or play favorites."

Spider nodded agreement. "That's what," he said laconically. "I aim to do my best. The sheriff would have stayed and hunted the hills over, if he had known who or what it was he was supposed to hunt for."

"He might have come and asked me," Vida hinted slyly.

"He knows we're plumb up against a mystery," Spider asserted, "and he ain't got the time to turn out and play detective. Shep and me is goin' to try our hands at that. If we get on to anything that looks like a clue, I'm s'posed to let 'im know."

"Oh. You're out looking for clues, are you?" Vida's tone was strongly tinged with sarcasm.

"Yeah, that's what. We thought we had some clues but they're in the discard. Since Burney's proved he never done it—"

"That'll take a lot more proof than he's furnished yet," Vida cut in again stubbornly. "Here's a clue you might pass along to the sheriff and see what he'll do about it: Burney came over here last night and tried to kill Poppy when he was asleep under the wagon. But he got hung up, trying to get at him. Burney reached in from the side and Poppy slept with his head up between the front wheels. He tore Poppy's shirt, and I started screaming when I thought he was going to tip the wagon over, so then he ran. He went down in the flat to where the sheep were bedded down and killed another dog. And he tried to kill Walt Smith. But I—"

Spider moved closer and his eyes sharpened as he stared down into her face. "How d' yuh know?" he snapped. "How do you know it was Burney?"

"How do I know? Because I saw him, that's how. And Poppy saw him too. He saw him when he backed out from under the wagon and started to run away in the moonlight. That was just a few minutes before the storm came up. You know how those thunder heads rolled up last night, without the moon clouding over beforehand. Or if you don't, I can tell you. It was bright moonlight right up to when it began

118

to thunder and lightning overhead.

"So I started off in the moonlight when the dog began barking and then yelped and quit, down there by the sheep. I had my gun and I was going to shoot if I got a chance. Then Walt began to holler, and I told him to run this way, and he sure did! He ran like a scared coyote and Burney was right after him. When they got close enough, I fired a couple of shots at Burney, and he ducked to one side and turned and headed back the other way. The moon was behind the clouds by that time, so I just caught glimpses of him in the lightning flashes. I don't think I hit him," she added apologetically.

"Are you sure it was Burney? Would you be able to swear to it in court?" Spider was still staring at her.

"Of course I'm sure! Do you think it's easy to mistake him for any one else? He wasn't more than fifty yards away when the lightning lit up everything and I shot at him. He was almost as plain as you are this minute."

"What time was that? It started in to lightning about half-past ten—"

"Well, it was the first bright flash that showed him up. It was moonlight when I left the wagon and then the storm rolled up in front of the moon. Poppy saw him—"

Spider turned and looked inquiringly at Shelton. "You know what time Burney came home?" he said.

"Oh, then you know he was gone last night!" Vida stood up, quivering for the hunt. Until then, she may have had a subconscious doubt of Burney's guilt, in spite of the evidence of her eyes. For when all was said and done, the sheriff's evidence had seemed terribly conclusive.

"Yeah, he was gone," Spider stated glumly.

"But he came back just after the storm started," Shelton cut in. "Spider and I were just getting ready to follow and see if we could find him. We'd made up our minds to watch Burney, and if he left the ranch last night, we'd be right on his trail, as Spider would say. But we didn't miss him until just before the storm came up, because he'd left a candle burning, after we'd all gone to bed. Spider got up and looked, and the light was out, so we went down and found out that his horse was gone—and that was while the

119

moon was still shining." He turned to Spider for confirmation. "Wasn't it, Spider?"

"Yeah, it was moonlight when we left the bunk house, and it clouded over and started to thunder and lightning while we was down at the corral," Spider stated fairly.

"Yes, that's right, Vida. That was just when you say you left the wagon here to go out where the sheep were. Well, we were at the corral and we were going to saddle up and come over here, anyway. Then it started to rain like all get-out. We were standing there, wondering if it would be worth while, when Burney came home. We saw him ride down the hill—the lightning was something fierce by that time—and we hustled back to the bunk house before he came up. We didn't want him to know that we were watching him, you see."

"And that would give Burney about fifteen or twenty minutes to ride ten miles," Spider pointed out grimly.

"You don't know how long he'd been gone?" Vida was puzzled and she showed it.

"It couldn't have been more than an hour or so," Shelton told her. "You see, I made an excuse to go up to the cabin just about nine o'clock—or maybe a little after. Burney was in bed, then, reading a novel by candlelight. He'd acted pretty gloomy all evening; didn't he, Spider? He didn't eat any supper, but sat and smoked and looked into the fireplace, as if he were thinking pretty hard about something.

"So when I saw him reading in bed, Spider and I kind of made up our minds that he had settled down for the night. We wanted to get some sleep if we could, because we meant to put in all of today looking around, whether Burney liked it or not. And then Spider got up and saw the light was out, and he went to the cabin to make sure—and Burney was gone."

"How about the other fellows?" Vida was putting bacon sandwiches in a flour sack, with the evident intention of spending the day in the hills.

"Oh, they've made up their minds that Burney don't know a thing about the killing. They're off riding in the other direction to-day," Spider took it upon himself to explain. "Shep and I just pulled out and never said a word to

120

anybody. I'm liable to git my time—but that'll be all right. I guess there's other jobs running around loose in the country, that I could sink my loop on. I might even herd sheep for a change," he bantered, the twinkle showing briefly in his eyes.

CHAPTER TWENTY-THREE

SHELTON GOES ON HIS OWN

WELL, if you're going into the hills, I'm going with you," Vida announced with determination. "I'm not afraid of Burney any more, and I'd just like to have a hand in rounding him up. I found out that a gun is bigger than he is, and he knows it. And I can shoot just as well as either of you. So I'm going."

"Oh, say! It's going to be frightfully hot," Shelton exclaimed anxiously. "And Spider says it will be rough going, and maybe we'll have to do a lot of climbing afoot."

"It won't be a bit hotter in the hills than it will be in this wagon," Vida declared. "And I thrive on rough going; so that's no argument at all."

"Well, of course we'd like awfully well to have you with us—" Shelton flushed and stammered at the last, because he had caught a significant twinkle in Spider's eyes.

"We ain't goin' after Burney," Spider explained. "We don't know what we're going after. That spook, maybe. Burney was home at the ranch when we left, puttering around the cabin. Anyway, it's a cinch he never killed your uncle. He couldn't. He was in Pocatello all that day."

"Well, I'll believe my own eyes quicker than I would the sheriff." Vida had a streak of stubbornness that was slow to yield.

"Well, I wouldn't want to doubt your eyes," drawled Spider, "but I sure believe the sheriff. And there was the coroner too. He seen Burney in Pocatello and talked with him. Him and the sheriff was both down there from Shoshone, and your herder went there after 'em, instead of waiting at Corona till they come up. No, we've got to look for some one else that's hiding out in these hills."

121

"There's last night too," Shelton reminded her. "Of course, it isn't possible that Burney could ride from here over to the Sunbeam in much less than an hour." This was not altogether second-hand wisdom gleaned from Spider's talk. Shelton was rather a keen thinker himself, when he settled himself down to it.

"But how could there be another man the size of Burney in the country and no one know it?" Vida came back at him. "I tell you I *saw* him."

"At night," said Spider patiently. "Every time he's been seen around your camp, it's been at night. Why, I could strap a pair of stilts onto my legs and fix up to look like Burney in the dark. Lord!" he ejaculated. "I believe I fell onto the answer to the whole blame thing!"

Vida looked at him strangely. Mentally she was seeing how plausible that solution was, after all. She herself had gone striding over this very country on crude, homemade stilts, just for fun when she was a child. Still—

"How would stilts make a man so strong in his hands?" she questioned, with a catch in her voice over the horror her words conjured; the horror of seeing her Uncle Jake lying there with his poor twisted neck.

"There's tricks to help a man seem a whole lot stronger than what he is," Spider told her vaguely. "My belief is, there's somebody prowling around these hills, trying to pin something onto Burney," he declared boldly. "Why, it'd be a cinch, the way he's been workin' it, only he can't be in two places at once, and he can't keep tabs on Burney and do his dirty work all at the same time.

"So Burney slips alibis over on him now and then, and that kinda spoils his play. Come on, folks! We'll see what we can figure out on this trail. Anyway, I'll bet money I've got the answer right here. I'll bet it's just a common-sized man we want to look for, that hates Burney and wants to get him in bad."

"But who'd want to?" Vida asked uncertainly. "It would take a man half crazy with hate to think up a scheme like killing sheep and—folks—that way, and making big tracks around over the country. He'd need a pair of Burney's boots to do that and where would he get them?" She brought the package of sandwiches over to Shelton to tie on his saddle. "That would take the worst kind of an enemy to plan a series of crimes like this."

"Well, it sure don't take much to start some men loping along the hate trail," Spider asserted confidently. "Lots of men hate Burney. He's so ungodly big, he's got a cinch in everything but a gun fight, and he's kinda queer in his ways, all right. He don't mix with folks, and he don't try to make friends with nobody, so he ain't got so awful many. Well, I'll go saddle up your pony and we'll drift—if you're bound to come along with us."

"Poppy's going to be out with the sheep all day and Walt Smith has a little camp of his own out there on the flat. I'd be here all alone—and honestly, I'd feel a lot safer with you boys."

That, of course, settled any reluctance to take her with them. She mounted the pinto pony which Spider saddled and led up to her and they rode toward the hills. After the heavy, pelting rain of the night before, there was no possibility of finding any tracks, and they loped along in silence for the most part until they reached the first real climb and were compelled to go slowly.

Vida was studying the mystery from the new angle which Spider had presented with his theory. For that matter, so were Shelton and Spider. On a long slope which they were climbing, Spider pulled a foot free of the stirrup, slid over in the saddle until he was resting mostly on one thigh, and sifted tobacco into a cigarette paper.

"Yes, sir, that accounts for pretty nearly everything," he said, apropos of their thoughts. "If we can locate that cave that Shep went prognosticating around in, I'll bet you good money we'll nab the gentleman that's been doing all the mischief. Chances are, that's where he hangs out. And between you and me, I've got a notion I could name the man. I won't, because I ain't dead sure, and it's a nasty proposition tacking a crime like that on a fellow till you're dead certain he done it.

"But there's one fellow, and only one that I know of, that would be just mean enough to frame up a deal like this and put it through. He's strong as a bull and he hates

123

Burney worse than a school-ma'am hates a worm down her back. He's on the dodge for a killing he done in Hailey a year ago last winter. It was Burney's evidence that put the diamond hitch on him—and he broke jail and ain't been seen since. He left word he'd git Burney and when he did he'd git him *right*."

"Would he be afraid of a gun?" Vida asked.

The twinkling devil showed in Spider's eyes when he looked at her.

"My experience is that most any man is afraid of a gun that's pointed at him," he informed her dryly. "Everybody knows that Burney never packs a gun, so the man I'm talkin' about couldn't very well produce one and go on acting the part of Burney. Savvy? And he wouldn't be crazy enough to git himself shot, either. It would be up to him to drift when any one started shootin', unless he wanted to give the whole deal away."

"Is he in this country, do you suppose?" Shelton studied the hills before them with frank curiosity.

"If he's the man, he sure must be in this country. You wouldn't suppose he was in South America, would yuh?"

Shelton flushed, glanced quickly at Vida, caught her smile and looked away. "Of course," he said stiffly, "I realize I must have sounded half-witted. Not that it matters, at all —but what I really intended to ask was whether he was known to be in this country." And with that he immediately dropped back behind the other two and gave Spider no opportunity to answer him, even if he wanted to do so.

They worked their way up the more open slopes until they attained what might be called the heart of the Haunted Hills. All about them the crags rose sheer above cañons whose roughness was hidden beneath the deep green of pines, mottled along the center with the lighter foliage of cottonwoods that told where flowed the tiny streams which never reached the desert beyond.

"It sure is a great place to hide out in," Spider observed once, when they stopped on a high, bare ridge and gazed out over the rugged terrain. "And it's an almighty poor place to find anybody in. It's just a case of ridin' by guess and by gosh and takin' a chance on runnin' acrost any-thing."

"What about the cave? Aren't you going to hunt around there?" Vida asked him somewhat diffidently. She might bully Shelton and assert her wider experience; she might order her own father about like a hired man, but here she yielded the leadership to Spider, who seemed perfectly competent to handle any situation which might arise.

Spider turned himself about in the saddle and looked back to where Shelton was following a few paces behind them, his hands clasped on the saddle horn and his handsome mouth pinched in at the corners.

"Sure, we're going to explore that cave—if we can find where it's at. Shep, he went and lost it out of his pocket the other day after he got through playin' with it. He ain't been able to find it yet." Since he had a theory which left Burney clear of guilt, Spider was finding it easier to joke over their search.

"It certainly isn't up in this high country," Shelton said shortly. "You know as well as I do that it's in a cañon that branches off the big one."

"I'll bet I could find it," Vida declared suddenly. "What kind of a place was it, Shep? On the outside, I mean? Did it open out onto a rocky knoll, like that one over there?" She pointed with her quirt.

"No, it didn't. It was under a ledge on the side of the cañon. It was down east of the ridge where I left you that day—and it went straight back like a long tunnel. Then there were branches, after one went in quite a long way." He looked at her unsmilingly. "And I might add," he observed, with studied politeness, "that my given name is Shelton—Shelt for short. Excuse me for mentioning it, but I have just lately learned that it is a very common practise in this country to name sheep dogs Shep."

Vida bit her lip. "Sheep dogs have more sense than lots of people," she retorted enigmatically and studied the hills frowningly. "And as for your cave, there are dozens of caves like that." She smiled across at Spider in a way that Shelton did not find at all agreeable to himself. "I could show you a dozen long tunnels that open under ledges in cañons.

125

The hills are full of them. Wasn't there anything else to remember it by, Mr. Sherman?"

Shelton twisted his lips ironically. "Why, yes," he replied, with malicious candor. "I lost old Dutch there and had to walk home. If you could just find the place where I lost Dutch, the cave is right close by. Just up the hill a stone's throw, in fact."

Vida's chin lifted at that, which heartened Shelton somewhat. He was not so pleased to see Spider's grin of amusement. But he was a good-tempered young man by nature and he forgot his small grudge the moment after it was satisfied. "By Jove!" he exclaimed. "If we could find that old Indian squaw again, she might know if there's anybody else living here in the hills."

"I thought you said she was crazy," Spider's enthusiasm seemed to conserve itself for his own ideas. "And blind," he added.

"Well, yes, she was, almost. But she knew soon enough when I got near her."

"If she's blind, she couldn't see him, and if she's crazy, we couldn't depend on anything she said. So what's the use? If you know any caves that might do for a hang-out, Vida, let's take a look at 'em. I brought candles along."

"I know lots of them. Not on this side, though." Vida examined the nearest bluffs critically. "Shelton's right about that—we'll have to get across this ridge and down into the big cañon somehow. It's just as though these hills were piled up all hot, and before they got cold they crumpled down on one side, which left lumps and hollows all through them. Over on the other side is where almost all the caves are, as far as I know."

That meant a wide detour, because they were already up so high in the hills that the cañons could not be crossed except afoot. Shelton wanted to return the way they had come and take the trail down into the cañon, but Spider did not pay much attention to his opinions or his wishes. After all, he was only a tenderfoot, Shelton told himself, and those two up ahead were Western to the bone. He felt their clannishness and became moody and silent, riding by himself whenever the roughness of the country would permit.

Thus they reached the lower country some distance apart, and in crossing a series of low ridges they became separated. Shelton, it must be admitted, had rather assisted in the separation by loitering behind a ridge and in letting Dutch climb at a slant that would eventually land him in the big cañon—or upon its rim, at least, where he trusted to luck to find a way down.

Once in the cañon of caves, he intended to do a little exploring on his own account. He had ridden with candles wrapped in a gunnysack and tied to his saddle ever since the day he had found the footprints in the cave, and he felt that he was not altogether helpless. If Vida wanted to stick with Spider, she certainly had his permission. A lot they cared about finding clues, so long as they could ride side by side and make eyes at each other, he told himself glumly.

Well, so far as he was concerned, they could wander where they pleased. He was out to solve the gruesome mystery of these hills, and he wasn't going to be sidetracked by Spider or any one else.

That being his mood, when he saw a spooky-looking gorge, all jutting ledges and with deep crevasses along the sides, he turned deliberately into it, in spite of the fact that it led straight away from the place where he had last seen Spider and Vida.

CHAPTER TWENTY-FOUR

ARGUMENT GETS NOWHERE

I T IS NOT WISE for a party to become separated in the wilderness. Shelton, born to the easy ways of policed streets with signs on the corners, and with countless ways of reaching home from any given point, had not heard of that unwritten law of the wild which commands a man to keep in touch with his companions or to have a meeting place arranged farther along. He went calmly about his own business, with no compunction whatever.

It never occurred to Spider and Vida, however, that Shelton was not following. They waited on top of the ridge, talking of many things. After a while, they rode back to where they could scan the long bare slope which they had just climbed; for Shep was green and there was no telling what might have happened.

They did not see anything of him, for the simple reason that he had already crossed the ridge lower down toward its point, hidden from them by a straggling growth of alders. They went back to the highest point and waited there, watching all the slopes. With his hands cupped for a megaphone, Spider yelled to the four quarters of the earth until he was purple.

They retraced their steps to where they had last seen Shelton and from there they tried to track him. They succeeded in following his trail halfway up the ridge, only to lose all trace of him in a patch of short, thick grass all matted together with last year's growth. Spider called him several things beside a tenderfoot, relieving his mind a little. He told Vida over and over how carefully he had warned Shep against wandering off by himself like this and getting himself lost.

They returned to the pinnacle and waited again, and watched the hills and cañons spread all about them, as an eagle must watch from his aerie. Spider repeatedly declared that they ought to go on and leave him out there. It would serve him right, he said, and learn Shep a lesson. But they lingered still, Vida insisting upon abiding by the law of the wild that stragglers must be accounted for before a party may continue its journey. Perhaps the law in itself would not have held Spider, if Vida had not been there to make the waiting pleasant. Also, he could not forget that somewhere this wilderness held concealed a man who would murder wantonly and without just cause.

"Aw," said Spider at last, when the sun hung high and hot over their heads, "there's no use waiting here any longer. Shep wouldn't have sense enough to come back where he missed us, anyway. He'd uh showed up long ago if he was coming. We've done our share and then some. We've waited here and hunted and watched a good two hours, and I've hollered my fool head off. If that fellow we're after is anywhere within ten mile of us, he knows just where we're located by this time. Let's get on over the other side of

128

the mountain and take a look at them caves."

"But I can't see where Shelton could have gone to!" Vida complained nervously. "He's always so considerate of other people's feelings, and so polite—I'm sure he wouldn't deliberately go off and leave us like this."

"Well, my experience is, you never can tell what a pilgrim is going to do," Spider declared. "Shep's probably aiming to bring in the murderer by his high lonesome."

"I don't think so. I'm sure something must have happened to him," Vida insisted. "If we could only *do* something—"

"Let's go on back to camp." Spider had made that suggestion four or five times in the last two hours without any success, but he made it again in the faint hope that Vida would change her mind. "This ain't no business for a girl, anyway—trackin' down a murderer. What we need out here is a posse. We'll go on back, and I'll get Spooky and Jim, and if Shep ain't back by that time, we'll bring a pack outfit over and comb these hills proper. I guess Shep was a little sore, the way I kinda throwed it into him. I sure never meant—"

"Oh, I know all that. I'm as much to blame as you are." Vida spoke impatiently, tears close to her voice. "I don't see why you have to go back and get Spooky and Jim. I'm here and I can shoot. That's what will count if we meet him. I'm not so easily frightened as you may think. I must say I don't like the idea of your feeling as if you've got me on your hands to take care of. I'm used to doing my share of whatever is to be done. I went out and brought in Walt Smith last night when Burney, or whoever it was, was chasing him. Walt was scared silly. And he ran to me for protection."

"That don't say it's your place to stick around up here hunting a dangerous criminal," Spider retorted, honestly worried on her account.

"The place for me," said Vida sharply, "is where I decide I'm needed most. You needn't bother about me, at all. I'm quite capable of taking care of myself. Of course, I can see you don't want me along—"

"Aw, I never meant that atall! I don't know of anybody I'd rather have along," Spider recanted, his voice softening

129

unconsciously. "And I never meant that you're afraid. You sure have got most of the men skinned for nerve. I never seen a woman as nervy as you are." He paused and leaned a bit closer. "If there's anything I hate, it's a coward," he added guilefully. "All I meant was that I ain't as brave for you as you are for yourself. I dunno what I'd do if anything was to happen to you."

Vida was not schooled to coquetry. She bit her lip and looked away from him, across the uneven crests of the hills. She had no pert answer ready. She was acutely conscious of his hand behind her on the high cantle; it had almost an effect of an embrace. And she was unpleasantly conscious of her own awkwardness.

"Why, there's Shelton, away over there! Isn't it?" She pointed a slim, brown finger, not trying to hide her excitement. "It's a white horse, anyway. I'll bet he's headed for home."

Spider frowned and took away his hand. Even at two or three miles' distance Shep could be a confounded nuisance, it would seem, and interrupt just when he shouldn't.

"Yeah, it's him, all right," he conceded briefly. "Now you'll quit worrying' about him, maybe. He's all right, and you couldn't git to him under an hour unless you was to fly; so what'll we do? Follow him up or take a look around them caves?"

"Certainly I won't follow him." Vida started her pony, forward, wondering why she should feel such a sudden depression of spirits. "I guess he doesn't want our company very badly or he'd have stayed with us. It's awfully hot. Let's hunt for a spring. Shelton has my lunch on his saddle—"

"I got enough for both of us. It sure would hit the spot right now. We'll eat and then go hunt them caves."

Vida's interest in caves seemed to have dwindled considerably. Her eyes followed that white speck crawling along in the distance. "We'll have to go pretty near as far as Shelton has gone over that way to get where there are any caves that I know about," she said apathetically. "But we'll go, of course, after we rest a little."

She rode part way down the ridge in silence. "I just can't
130

make myself believe it wasn't Burney," she broke out abruptly. "A man with stilts on could make tracks—I can see how that would be easy enough, but—"

"But what?" Spider looked at her unsmilingly. He had thought her convinced. So far as he could see, she had been quite ready to accept his theory. It was like a woman, he thought, to fly back on an argument and have to go through the whole deal again. "What makes it so hard to believe?"

Vida twisted her slim body about in the saddle so that she faced him. Her eyes held a worried look.

"Oh, I hate this talking and talking and never getting anywhere," she protested impatiently. "But I just *can't* believe it wasn't Burney. The man I saw was big. Not just tall but *big*. He was so big he couldn't crawl under the wagon like a common man would, to get at Poppy. Of course, you might say that stilts would make it too awkward for him, but that doesn't account for everything, either. He woke me up, tilting the wagon up on one side, trying to crawl under between the wheels. Our brake sticks out quite a way, but still any common man could have gotten under easily enough.

"No, it was Burney. I *know* it was. When I saw him chasing Walt Smith, I knew him because it looked like Burney. He didn't run like a man on stilts—oh, you know yourself you wouldn't be fooled by any contraption like that. We're not after any common-sized man and I know it. And he doesn't live in any cave, either. He lives right over at the Sunbeam ranch. It's all foolishness, hunting through all the caves. Even if he were in one, we couldn't get him. He'd be a fool to hole up in a cave with only one entrance and he'd see us coming with our lights."

"Why didn't you say in the first place that's the way you felt about it?" Spider's voice was hard and even, with a grating quality seldom heard in it.

"Sometimes a person feels things without realizing it. I knew all the time I didn't feel right about your stilt theory, or the caves, either."

"If you don't want to hunt through the caves, what's the use of going on?" Spider pulled his horse to a stand, his face dark with anger. "I didn't know we was just out here

131

on a picnic. I'll take yuh back to camp and then I'll have a free hand to look where I want to look. Come on—I'll want a little time before dark."

"Oh, well, if you're going to get mad about it," she yielded the point, though her own eyes were burning with anger. "I'll go through the caves, if that's what you want. But I know it won't be a bit of use."

"I don't want you to go through the caves. I kept tellin' you all the time I didn't. It ain't safe for a girl and I don't want to be held up lookin' after yuh." Then, just because he had lost his temper, he spoiled his last chance of sending her back. "If it was Burney, you'd be dead safe, and I wouldn't need to worry a minute about yuh," he said. "It's just because it ain't him—"

"It seems to me you know altogether too much about who it is and who it isn't!" snapped Vida, and sent her pony on down the hill. To tell the truth, she did not mean anything by that, except that she hated his being so positive.

But Spider turned white around the lips and nostrils and, just as Shelton had done earlier that day, he fell back a couple of rods in the rear. Had he not known that she really was not safe in those hills alone, he would have left her to herself. As it was, he made a compromise between his anger and his conscience by keeping her in sight while he remained so far behind that she would be obliged to stop and wait for him deliberately before there could be any further speech between them.

Once or twice Vida looked back very cautiously over her shoulder and saw that Spider had no intention of overtaking her. For this she was a highly indignant young lady. Here was the second escort to desert her in the wildest part of the Haunted Hills. Shelton, she admitted to herself, had some reason for riding off by himself. There was no question of safety then, because Spider had been with her. But now Spider was doing the same thing. And if he really believed she wasn't safe alone, why did he lag along behind like that? Well, all right; if he wanted to keep his distance, she's make it easy for him.

So she urged her pony down that hill at a shuffling trot, and when he was at the bottom, she put him into a lope.

She felt hateful and she meant to act just as hateful as she felt. No Sunbeamer need think he could whistle her to his heels! He wanted to hunt through the caves, did he? Very well, if he kept on her trail, she would lead him to all the caves she knew, and he could hunt through them to his heart's content. Much good it would do him, with the murderer hanging out at the Sunbeam ranch all the while!

CHAPTER TWENTY-FIVE

TRAILS MEET

VIDA was a girl and she was given to moods. Though she was accustomed to hard living and to worrying over many things—accustomed even to tragedy in a small way —nevertheless she had been deeply stirred by the outrages on her family. In the past forty-eight hours she had run the gamut of emotions, and nerves are tricky things at best. Now, because Shelton's desertion had upset her more than she would have cared to confess, even to herself, and she had quarreled with Spider chiefly because he was partly to blame for Shelton's mood, she had pushed into the background of her mind the real object of their quest.

To lead Spider through the hills, to dodge into this cave and that cave ahead of him—making sure always to keep ahead of him—now became a matter of first importance. To make him think he had permanently lost sight of her while she watched from some hiding place in the rocks would give her real satisfaction, in the mood she was in.

As for Burney the killer, she thought of him often, while she was riding through the wildest places, and sent uneasy glances around her. But she had her gun safe in its holster at her hip, and the belt sagged with loaded cartridges; and Burney was afraid of a gun. So she put the unwelcome thought of him from her and went on showing her contempt for Spider as a leader.

It is safe to say that not one of the three ever dreamed that fate was leading him that day. Yet Vida's seemingly aimless riding and Shelton's piqued wanderings served to

133

bring the whole mystery to a crisis within the next hour or so.

Fate—or whatever name you wish to call it by—sent Shelton C. Sherman ambling down a cañon up which Burney himself was riding slowly, purposefully, saving his big horse deliberately, that he might get from him all of his speed and endurance, should the need come later.

Shelton stopped short in a sandy draw, much astonished at the meeting. Burney stopped also, perhaps similarly astonished, though that would be hard to determine simply by looking at him. It seemed as though Burney, having been given the normal amount of human emotions, had to spread them out very thin to fill his great self; so that they reached the surface of his face so diluted as to be scarcely discernible. That, at any rate, was what Shelton often thought of him.

His little eyes twinkled sharply at the young man who was supposed to be some place else, but they failed to reveal any expression of his personal attitude toward the meeting. They always did twinkle, even when he looked at inanimate objects. Shelton had often wondered at that. And although he searched Burney's face now for some clue to his mood, he knew that it was of no use.

Burney had one peculiar trait which caused a good deal of discomfort amongst his men. He did not ask many questions and yet he had the knack of squeezing one dry of information. He certainly squeezed Shelton dry, in the ten minutes which they spent there talking. Where he had been, Shelton told truthfully—because somehow Burney's eyes compelled him to do so. What had happened at the Williams camp last night, and what Vida and her father thought about it; where he and Spider and Vida had started for that morning, and why; Spider's theory of the man who wore stilts and a pair of big boots fastened on somehow to make tracks like Burney's; everything, in fact, that Shelton C. Sherman knew about the affair, he told—just because Alec Burney sat there on his big horse and stared down at him with an expectant look in his little eyes. It was as if they were always saying, "Well, well, is that all?"

Afterward, Shelton cursed himself for his imprudence.

134

Even while he was speaking, he was troubled by the guilty conviction that these things should be kept to himself. Why he told them he could not understand; certainly he was not given to blabbing everything he knew. He felt helpless, almost hypnotized, under that steady stare. So, right or wrong, Burney heard things that must have surprised him.

"Whereabouts was they headed for when you left 'em?" Without shifting his gaze from Shelton's face, Burney asked almost his first question. Apparently he wished to have certain details made as clear as possible.

"I imagine they were going to some caves that Vida knows about. They meant to try and find the one I was in when I saw the tracks. The tracks of your boots," Shelton explained obediently. "And of the big bear tracks too. They think maybe they'll find some clue around there. It will be pure luck if they do find it. I tried to take Spider there the other day and I couldn't find it anywhere." He wondered if it was just his imagination that Burney looked slightly relieved at that statement. "We didn't have any better luck finding the squaw I met, who said—" Shelton stopped in some embarrassment.

"Said what?"

"Said she—er—knew—your father. She said—".

"Did they go straight up into the hills from the Williams camp?"

"Just as straight as we could. I left them as we were climbing up over that long ridge."

Burney glanced up at the sun. "You better go on home," he said, in his high, querulous voice. "You can work on the corral, so we can throw in some stock I want the boys to bring in. I'm going to see Williams. I'll be back in a couple of hours. If Spooky's there, tell him to have dinner ready when I git there." He gave Shelton another sharp glance, seemed to hesitate, and rode on past without talking.

So they separated, the young man going down the cañon toward the more open country, and the other riding up into the heart of the wilderness.

When he had ridden a few rods, Shelton looked back over his shoulder. He caught Burney looking back also, with something furtive in his glance. In some confusion, Shelton

135

faced to the front again and rode on, but with his mind busy with the man behind him.

If Burney were going to the Williams camp, what was he doing, riding up this cañon? This would make the way longer as well as rougher; a useless detour, so far as Shelton could determine. If he were not going to Williams camp, why should he make that bald statement? Burney was not in the habit of volunteering information to any one except when it was necessary to do so. It certainly was not necessary now.

Uneasiness grew to suspicion in Shelton's mind. Why had Burney been so particular about wanting to know just where Vida and Spider were going? What was that to Burney? Shelton rode a few rods farther, thinking hard. He could have bitten off his tongue for having told Burney so much. What if Burney really were the killer—a homicidal maniac that killed whatever was within reach when the fit came on him?

A dryness came into Shelton's throat. He turned impulsively in the sandy draw and rode back up the cañon as quietly as he could. Before him was the dreadful vision of the scattered carcasses of dead sheep mysteriously crushed and broken, and the twisted corpse of a man lying cold under the stars; and of Vida and Spider, riding together over the ridge, talking, laughing maybe, forgetting the danger they might meet in the hills. He shivered, though the day was hot.

CHAPTER TWENTY-SIX

A NIGHTMARE COMES TRUE

HALFWAY UP a forbiddingly barren gulch, Vida stopped and looked inquiringly behind her. She had been riding rather slowly since she had turned into this small cañon, and it seemed to her that Spider should have overtaken her ten minutes ago. She was certain that he had seen her turn off from the larger cañon which they had been following with a good two hundred yards of space between them.

For an hour she had played hide and seek with him

in a quiet way, and in the playing had recovered her usual calm self-reliance. The horror of the past two days was there still, but now she felt herself quite able to cope with it and with any other emergency which might arise.

Now that her anger with him had subsided and she could be perfectly just, she rather wished that Spider would over-take her. She wanted to tell him that after all it might not be Burney who had done the murder. It had occurred to her that a man with stilts strapped on his legs—low ones, of course; not more than ten or twelve inches high—would find it awkward to crawl under a wagon in the dark; and that any strong man, heaving upward with his bent back to lift the weight, could tilt their camp wagon.

She realized now that the imagination is prone to play tricks upon a person whose nerves are strained to the snap-ping point. The first thing that Poppy would think of when he woke up like that, with some one clawing at him, would be Burney. And when he saw a man rise up and look about seven feet tall, of course he'd think it was Burney. And believing the marauder to be the boss of the Sunbeam, she herself would take it for granted that it was Burney whom she saw. Given the height, the rest would seem perfectly natural.

She would tell Spider all this and eat a little humble pie. It would do her good, she guessed. She wished that she could eat humble pie for Shelton, but he had put himself effec-tually out of her reach by going back to the ranch. She certainly would not ride away over there—that would be too abject a surrender.

And as for Spider, she certainly did not mean to go out of her way to meet him. He'd think she hunted him up because she was scared, or because her conscience hurt her. And neither would be true, because she certainly was not afraid of anything and her conscience was clear of guilt. She had not run away from Spider. He had simply lagged behind, which was no way for a deputy sheriff to act.

Again she looked behind her and she shivered without quite knowing why she did so. She had stopped in the cañon to wait for Spider, and at first she had been looking back expectantly, thinking that she would presently see

137

him ride around the bend. But now she felt as though something horrible was going to appear from behind that jagged point of rocks.

She kicked her pony in the flanks and rode on hurriedly, looking for a way out of the gulch. She felt the blood creeping back to her heart which began pounding heavily. Where was Spider? Why didn't he come? Was he lying somewhere with his neck broken and twisted in that horrible manner? She tried not to believe that such a thing could happen here in broad daylight, to a man who had a six-shooter and a rifle, and would certainly use one or the other if he were attacked. Still, the ghastly picture of him lying so persisted in appearing before her.

She rode on as fast as her pony could go, and she kept looking over her shoulder, eyes wide with terror. Never before had Vida felt that indefinable fear of something she could not see, though she had ridden alone in these hills many times since she was a child. She remembered once when she had shot a mountain lion, how scared she had been, but it had been a perfectly normal, healthy fear lest her bullets should fail to do their work and the wounded lion might claw her.

Now she tried to shake off this nameless horror that had seized her, tried to reason with her unreasoning dread of something which she could neither hear nor see. But all the while she kept thinking of the *something* that had followed Shelton and Spider and the others—the something they could not name but had felt behind them in the dark. She had not thought much about it before; indeed, save those few minutes of terror in the wagon, when half awake she had envisioned a warlock, she had mentally pooh-poohed the ghost story, half suspecting it of being some obscure joke such as cowboys are prone to invent.

But this was early afternoon, and she herself was experiencing the prickling of her scalp such as Shelton had described. Had she not been afraid to do so, she would have turned then and ridden back to find Spider. She felt that she would have borne any repulse, any reproach, only so he was there beside her, rough and tanned and efficient, with his two guns.

138

But she couldn't turn back. She was afraid. Nothing could induce her to turn and ride down that gulch. Instead, she struck her pony sharply with the quirt and went clattering over the rocks in a way to rouse the echoes and let them clamor of her whereabouts to any one within a quarter of a mile.

But that could not go on. She saw how the gulch was drawing together ahead of her, and let the pony slow to a walk. Unless the cañon widened just around the next point, she would be trapped. Or if she could get up the bluff, she reasoned swiftly, she might follow back along the edge until she saw Spider, and then call down to him and have him join her up there.

Longingly she gazed up at the frowning rock ledges above her head. Up there, she believed, she would be safe. Even the scattered fringes of serviceberry bushes and buckbush looked reassuring, as if they could protect her from something that was creeping up on her from behind. But there was no place along the cañon wall where her pony could climb, and Vida caught herself sobbing dryly as she rode along, seeking a way out.

Then her terror mastered her completely. In a sudden panic, she pulled up and slid off the horse, ran to the shadowed side of the gulch and began to climb. When she had reached a ledge that stood out flat-surfaced from the steeper front of the ravine wall, she stopped and stood panting, while she watched with straining eyes the rough trail she had ridden over but a few moments ago.

Something was coming stealthily, swiftly, surely upon her trail. She knew it, even though she could see nothing but the black, barren rocks and the stunted bushes and wavering heat line, where the sunlight struck full upon the opposite wall.

And then a huge, black head, bare and tousled, peered cautiously around a sharp projection of rock; waited there motionless for a long minute and moved forward, pushed by the broad shoulders of a figure grown horribly familiar. Even at that distance Vida fancied that she could see the little, twinkling eyes as they searched the cañon.

He came on with swift, stealthy strides that c

forward with amazing speed; a noiseless, swinging trot that was half a lope and that would in the long run, outstrip a horse. This was no man on stilts, making himself tall to look like Burney. This was the giant himself, reverted to the cave man hunting down his prey. He ran, then stopped and crouched behind a bowlder. She could see only the slope of his shoulders as he waited there.

With a sob suppressed in her throat, Vida ducked into a crevice and began to climb. It was like her dream come true, except that in her dream the cañon wall was smooth and perpendicular, while in reality it was broken and not too steep, if she chose her way very carefully. The rest was horribly true to the nightmare, with Burney stealing swiftly along, looking here and there and everywhere for her.

In the crevice she was hidden from him, but she dared not stay there. He would come upon her pony and know that she had taken to the cañon side. He would even know which side, because the opposite wall overhung the gulch, leaning outward so slightly that it offered no hiding place beneath. He would not puzzle one minute over her whereabouts. He would know. And he would climb up after her. With his long arms and his long legs and his enormous strength to lift him up the bluff, he would climb ten feet while she was toiling five.

She struggled upward, cursing the denim riding skirt that caught on sharp points and impeded her progress. She tried to keep her wits and to climb intelligently, and she kept to an angle that would take her farther down the cañon. If she reached the top, she would be nearer to Spider and safety—for even though Spider saw it was his boss who was after her, surely he would shoot—and shoot to kill.

Then a rock which she had seized to pull herself across a treacherous space of loose earth gave way beneath her fingers and went clattering down the wall, bouncing off ledges and gathering speed and noise as it went. Breathless she watched it. She could not see Burney just then, but she knew that he was down there and that his little, twinkling eyes were seeking, seeking. She knew that he would hear the rock and would know that she had loosened it in ier flight from him.

She shut her eyes, sick with fancying what would happen then. Like Shelton in the cave, she never once thought of using her gun, though it swung heavy on her hip and even hindered her movement when she pressed close against a ledge. She was like Walt Smith, fleeing from Burney in the moonlight. In her nightmare, she had not dreamed of shooting, and now when reality was more horrible than any dream, she still did not remember that one means of defense. Flight, primitive, wild flight seemed to her the only possible escape from those monstrous, clutching hands.

Spider—where was Spider? Why didn't he come? Her pony, left alone down there, suddenly snorted. She heard the clatter of rocks as he whirled and fled back down the cañon. Then she opened her eyes and looked, for the sounds were almost directly beneath her. Down below her the pinto came galloping, fright making him sure-footed among the scattered rocks that strewed the bottom.

Behind him, running with great leaps that ate up the space between them, came Burney. Bareheaded, evil-faced, intent on the chase. The pony ran into a jumble of rocks, stumbled, recovered himself and swerved to find an easier passage. Like a huge gorilla, Burney leaped directly into his path. Like the gorilla his long arms shot out and caught the pony around the neck. He gripped it, leaning, straining his great body against the pinto's shoulder. Vida hid her face against the rock. Her knees sagged under her with ghastliness of the thing.

But her own danger galvanized her into action again. She did not look below—she did not dare. Instead, she looked up and took heart, when she saw how close she was to the top. Another five minutes and she would be on the rim, unless the bluff merely receded and went on up, as might be the case. Instinctively she nerved herself for that disappointment and climbed doggedly, desperately. She would get to the top—she *had* to! And she would run and run until she found Spider.

She had climbed another thirty feet, perhaps, when she heard the half shout, half scream that told her she had been discovered. Still she did not look back. She only climbed the faster. There was something maniacal in the sound. She sensed it even in her fright and knew that Burney was crazy —an insane giant hunting her down.

Sane, she would not have feared him; or not nearly so much. She would have felt that by sheer will power she could dominate even his bigness. But a crazy man could not be dominated by any thing save superior force. So she climbed and climbed with a frantic haste that never stopped for breath. She heard him knocking rocks loose, down there below, as he lunged up the cañon wall after her.

With a dry sob of thankfulness she topped a broad ledge and found herself upon comparatively level ground. Though it was rough enough to prevent swift flight, it looked smooth and safe after that terrible climb. For a moment she stood still, straining her eyes to see far down the cañon, looking for help. She found that she was on a narrow tongue of a ridge, and that she could look down upon either side. And in the farther cañon, which was strange to her, a horseman was ambling along at a little jog trot.

Though he was far away, Vida gave a sob of relief. It was Spider, and though it was doubtful if he could hear her, she called to him at the top of her voice and started running down the ridge, looking for a way down into that cañon.

From behind her came a hoarse, chortling laugh, so close that she glanced back in fresh terror. She saw the bare head of the giant show over the top of the last ledge, and with a scream she ran on down the ridge. Stumbling, tripping over rocks, she yet managed somehow to keep her feet and to keep going.

It was her nightmare, magnified fourfold by the small details one could never imagine in advance. For there was no way down into the cañon up which the Spider was riding. Or if there were, she did not dare take time to look for it. She kept running, knowing instinctively that if she stopped and tried to climb off the ridge to get to Spider, she would be trapped on the rim. Her only recourse then would be to throw herself off the edge—and it was life she was fighting for, not death at the foot of a cliff.

The ridge sloped sharply downward toward the point where the cañons had forked. Even as she ran, she remembered that she had noticed the bare slope of this dividing ridge and had even thought of riding up it to get a clear view of the surrounding country. Why hadn't Spider ridden up here, instead of keeping to the cañon—and the wrong one at that?

She did not look again behind her. She knew too well what she would see. She knew that if she saw Burney on the level, coming after her with those terrible, long strides, his twinkling little eyes fixed greedily upon her, the sight would paralyze her. So she ran and did not look back.

CHAPTER TWENTY-SEVEN

NO MORE MYSTERY

W HEN A MAN has spent nearly all of his life in the wilderness, certain of his faculties attain a high state of development; unless, of course, he is one of those incompetents who never does grow up to fill the requirements of his vocation. Spider was not an incompetent. He had learned to keep his eyes open and to rise instinctively to an emergency. Though he had lost Vida in the cañon it was because he had not suspected her of delicately trying to evade him. He had kept to the logical course, which was up the main ravine.

Neither was he greatly concerned over her welfare; he had too great a confidence in her ability to take care of herself, and he believed himself to be within shouting distance of her; which he had been until she turned up the side gulch and so passed completely out of touch with him. But even if he did not worry about her, he kept his eyes open and let no living thing move unseen within his range of vision. He saw Vida the instant she came out upon the crest of the ridge and he saw too that she was afoot and running from something.

Instinctively he knew what that something was and he dug the spurs into his horse and tore up the cañon, looking for a way up to where she was. There was no way that a horse could travel, and he jumped off and started scrambling up the rocks, much as Vida had done upon the other side of the ridge.

Once, when he was feeling for a handhold above him, where the cliff was almost straight, he heard a shout on the ridge above him. It sounded like Burney's high-pitched voice raised in command to some one. It seemed odd that Burney should be up there with Vida, since he had been at the ranch that morning with no apparent intention of leaving.

It did not seem odd to Shelton, however, who was climbing the other side of the ridge, having glimpsed Vida when she reached the top. Being a tenderfoot and therefore not credited with too much intelligence, he had immediately swung old Dutch to the bluff and forced him up it until a sheer rock wall stopped him. Dutch was puffing and blowing and couldn't have gone any farther, anyway, but Shelton did not worry about that. He had made a fair start up the hill without using his own energy and he felt that it was so much clear gain.

He clutched a splinter of rock, pulled himself up half his length, and looked over the ledge upon baked soil that still sloped steeply up to the crest. By sheer muscular strength he drew himself up over the smooth, black rim and ran up the steep slope on his toes until another ledge blocked the way and he must climb again foot by foot, clinging with his hands and his feet to the face of the rock.

He was still a few feet from the top when he heard Vida scream, and close upon her voice came the hoarse bellowing cry he had heard twice before. His breath caught in his throat at the sound, but he went on, climbing like a madman.

It seemed to him hours that he spent on that ledge, toiling upward with Vida's shriek and that other horrible cry ringing in his ears. It seemed to him that he made no headway at all, but climbed and climbed in one spot. Yet he found himself miraculously on the ridge, running up the bare crest of it toward a titanic struggle of some sort; just what it signified, he could not at first determine.

He did not see Vida anywhere, and when he realized that she was not involved in the battle, he slowed a little, drawing the breath gaspingly into his starved lungs. Then he saw her lying all crumpled in a heap where she had fallen on the stunted grass. He sprang forward, lifted the girl in his arms and ran with her to a group of great bowlders with bushes growing between. In the shade of a buckbush he laid her down, crushed his big hat under her head for a pillow and turned back to do what he could.

144

Close to the spot where Vida had fallen, a mighty battle was taking place; two giants of men whose breath came in great gasps while they strained and struggled. Panting, at first blankly uncomprehending, Shelton drew near and watched the amazing spectacle. There was Burney fighting doggedly, silently—fighting for his very life. And there was another Burney—and yet not Burney at all—fighting with harsh animal snarls of rage and the lust for killing; fighting not for his own life but for the lives of these others.

He was dressed in Burney's old clothes—Shelton remembered the gray striped trousers which Burney sometimes had worn; tattered now, torn short off at the hairy knees of the giant. He was like Burney in size and general outline of face and figure, and yet his face was the face of an animal, with its protruding jaw and receding forehead and broad, flat nostrils. His eyes were little and twinkling and set deep under his bushy brows. His arms were hairy, his legs were hairy and his feet, which were bare, were huge, misshapen things with queer-looking toes that spread wide apart as he braced his foot upon the ground, trying to throw Burney.

While he stared, Shelton began to understand many things that had been fogged in mystery. Here was the answer to the puzzle. Here was the thing that had followed him through the desert in the dark; the foot that made the bear track which he had found beside the little stream and in the cave. Here was the killer of sheep and dogs—and of Jake Williams; the monstrous shape that had tried to get in the wagon that night and could not, because the door was too small.

A wave of physical nausea surged over Shelton at the thought of this great savage trying to get at Vida. It passed, and a spasm of terror seized him, as he realized suddenly that the fight was not going as it should. Though Burney's strength was prodigious, the strength of this other was something beyond human calculations.

Step by step, inch by inch, Burney was being beaten back, borne down beneath this great beast of a man. Great sweat drops stood on his face. His teeth were clenched in a frozen snarl. As he strained, the cords stood out like small ropes on his neck. Slowly, slowly, his knees were bending beneath that

145

terrific pressure. His back seemed likely to be broken, strong though it was.

The huge hairy hands of the Thing were reaching, reaching —the great talonlike fingers were spread and tensed for the death clutch. The snarl broke suddenly into a scream to freeze one's blood; the scream which Shelton had heard behind him in the dark, the scream that had terrified him in the cave. And on the echoes of that scream came a groan, wrenched from Burney's throat in his agony.

Shelton sprang forward then, caught the huge beast man by the throat and tried to pull him off Burney. With one heave of the great shoulder and a catlike twist of his back, he threw Shelton off. Shelton tried slugging and felt as though he were lashing out at one of those black bowlders scattered along the ridge. He tore at the huge, hairy hands and knew that he must have seemed like a five-year-old child trying to fight his daddy. Try as he might, his lusty young strength could avail nothing.

For one instant Burney's eyes met his in a desperately intent start. "Shoot!" gasped Burney, as the hairy hands clamped down on his throat.

Automatically Shelton obeyed. He did not know how he got his gun from the holster nor how he aimed. The roar of the shot was muffled against the monster's side. He recoiled, swayed on his great hairy limbs and sank to his knees; balanced there uncertainly for a moment and toppled over upon his side. And all at once the Thing was no more than a great heap of flesh, grotesquely clothed in Burney's coat and trousers.

Burney removed the gripping hands—relaxed now and helpless—and staggered to his feet. With a trembling palm, he wiped the sweat from his forehead and stared stupidly down at what lay there on the ground. He looked up, took a staggering step and laid a huge paw on Shelton's shoulder for support.

"Is the girl all right?" he mumbled dazedly, his high-pitched voice trembling. "I saw him—after her. I run my horse—and got here just in time." He looked at the dead giant and his face clouded with something close to sadness.

Spider came trotting up, weak and panting with exhaustion

from the climb he had made. He stared at the Thing on the ground, stared at Burney and shifted his gaze to Shelton, who stood with his six-shooter still dribbling a little smoke from its barrel. "Well, I'll be damned," gasped Spider under his breath.

"I think we better go over here and sit down in the shade," Shelton suggested rather shakily. "I feel about all in, right now. I think we all are." He turned and led the way to where Vida still lay beside the buckbush. Ignoring the other two, he knelt and took her small, brown hands in his, stroking them gently. With a touch that was a caress he laid his fingers on her temple. She lay as she had lain the day before, lightly breathing, deeply unconscious. He sat back on his heels and looked at her, glancing up at the others.

"I think we'd just better let her be for the present," he said softly, his breathing uneven from the experience of the last few minutes. "She fainted yesterday, you know, and she was all right afterwards and able to come out here to-day. My sister has these spells when anything upsets her too much."

Spider nodded. Shelton rose and found himself a level place on a near-by rock and sat down, wiping his face with his handkerchief.

Spider was looking curiously from Burney to the dead giant. "You must uh knowed about him all the time," he said abruptly, jerking his head toward the trampled battle scene. "He's got on your coat and pants."

Burney lifted his chin from his heaving chest and stared somberly at the dead.

"Sure, I knew about him," he admitted dismally. "I never knew he was dangerous though—not till he commenced killin' sheep. Even then I didn't think—he'd tackle a human being. He's always been harmless. Just—kind uh simple-minded and wantin' to live around in caves like an animal. He never hurt nobody before. It must uh growed on 'im, kind uh, after killin' them sheep."

He heaved a great sigh, took his handkerchief from his pocket, wiped his face and then shook it out and went over and spread it over the dead face that was still snarling.

He came back and sat down heavily on the rock near the

147

two. "I wish we could keep this thing quiet," he said gloomily, after a silence. "Uh course he wasn't responsible for what he done, and he wasn't hardly human, but he—" His face flushed darkly. "I s'pose you'd call 'im a half-brother of mine," he said, with a shamed kind of defiance. "My dad was a squaw man up in Montana. I s'pose maybe you've heard that, Spider. Breed Jim knew about it."

"Yeah, I heard somethin' about it," Spider admitted, in a tone meant to be carelessly indifferent. "Never paid no attention to that. Hell, the West is full uh men that had Injun wimmen. Used to be damned lonesome livin' out here in them old days."

"That was when I was just a kid," Burney went on more easily. "My mother was a fine woman. Too fine for the life she had to live, I guess. I wasn't more'n five years old when she died." He glanced reluctantly over to the inert heap on the ground. "Way it happened, him and his squaw got mixed up with a grizzly bear. My old man was hurt so he died. The kid that was born afterwards was—him." He tilted a thumb expressively.

"He never was right, not from the very start. Soon as he could walk, he had the ways of an animal more'n a human. Yuh see his feet—a good deal like a bear's. Old Mary—that's the squaw—she just about worshiped him. And when he growed up and took to the hills, she went with 'im and lived the way he lived and took care of him best she could."

Shelton glanced toward the dead, shuddered and looked away. It seemed terrible to him now that he had taken the life of a human being—even a half-human creature such as that Thing had been. He looked at Burney strangely, wondering what were his thoughts, and whether he felt any hidden resentment toward the killer.

Burney glanced up and met Shelton's eyes, and answered the unspoken question.

"Maybe I hadn't ought to be, but I'm glad he's gone," he said soberly. "Uh course, it was him or me, that last minute. I ain't thinkin' of that, nor what he done over to the Williams camp. But he's always hung over my head like a—a disgrace. A Thing like that hadn't oughta be left alive. The squaw'd oughta done away with it, when it was born.

148

I always felt that way about it, even when I was a kid.

"He couldn't talk—not words you could get any sense of. The squaw, she could always make out what he wanted, and she waited on him hand and foot—and him just gruntin' at her. There was something about him always give me the shivers. But I took as good care of 'em both as I could. I used to send money up to a feller in the Bitter Root that knew where they hung out. And he bought things for 'em.

"Then the squaw found her eyesight was goin', and one way and another she trailed him off down here where I was. He—" Burney nodded toward the corpse "—never showed up in daytime, so nobody never knowed anything about him, back up in Montana, except this man that used to be my old dad's partner.

"He died a couple uh years ago, and that's when Mary, she struck out with—*him*—and come on down here. Traveled nights, she said, so there didn't nobody see him. Mary always hid him away when he was little. She never wanted him seen. It made her sore to have folks know he was— *different*. She used to hide him like a deer hides her fawn. So they located here in these hills and I packed grub to 'em myself, nights." Burney gave a deep sigh, as though the burden had taxed all his strength and fortitude.

"Us fellows would uh stood right by yuh, if you'd told us about it," said Spider, with gruff sympathy. "We could uh helped, instead of yawping around about a spook. We'd uh kept our faces shut if we'd uh had any idee—"

"I know you would. But it wasn't a thing a feller wants to tell unless he's obliged to. I never thought he'd harm a soul," he repeated defensively. "I dunno what ever made him start in killin' sheep fer Williams—he must uh got the notion they was enemies. I done my best to git Williams to move back away from here. I s'pose I'd oughta told him why. But I didn't and so I'm responsible for a man's death." He humped forward, brooding over the tragedy.

"I tried to git the squaw to pull out," he went on, as if he were pleading the case with his conscience sitting in judgment. "I told her he was gittin' to act queer—when he commenced follerin' you boys—and he wasn't safe. I told her the sheriff would take 'im and shut 'im up in jail, if he got

149

to botherin' anybody. But you can't," he complained, "budge an Injun, if they don't want to do a thing. Well," he added justly, "there wasn't much she could do. Her eyesight was about gone, and she's old and kind uh crippled up, and she couldn't foller 'im around and keep 'im outa mischief. I guess she done the best she could.

"I went to Pocatello to see a doctor and try and find out what could be done for him. I'd heard about operations on the brain that'd change a person's disposition, and didn't know but what something could be done with him to make him quieter and keep him from wanting to kill things. I got uneasy when he commenced killin' sheep.

"Well, I didn't go soon enough. I'd oughta had him tended to when I first growed up and seen what he was like. But he seemed so harmless—and it would of been hell to cage him up—and I hated to have folks know about him. It's bad enough," he said doggedly, "to be so all-fired big you're pointed at on the streets, like you was a side show broke loose; and to feel you're different, and to have folks think you're a whole lot more different than what you are. They don't realize that I'm just a *man*—just like everybody else—and that just being bigger don't make me feel any different. If folks knowed I was related to a Thing like that, they'd think I was some kinda beast myself. I tried to do what was right by him, but I wanted some kind of fair show myself."

"Well, I guess you've got it coming, if anybody has," said Spider, after a thoughtful silence. "You'll sure git it from me. If we could do something with the body," he ventured tentatively, without looking at Burney, "I don't see why anybody'd need to know there'd ever been such a—person."

Burney lifted his bent head and looked at Spider almost eagerly. Then his face dulled again. "There's the girl," he said.

"Oh, say! You mustn't worry about Vida. She's perfectly wonderful." Shelton caught Spider's sardonic glance and his sunburned face turned even redder. "She's what you'd call the real goods. She never would say a word. If you could just manage to—to bury him secretly—"

"His cave's just down below," Burney said. "One of 'em, anyway. We could put him in there. We better hurry, if

150

we're going to do anything; if you think we can and it would be right. There's that murder—"

"Well, there won't be any more. And it won't be the only killing that never was accounted for," Spider said grimly. "We'll let Shep tell the girl about it, so she won't worry no more, or be scared. And what the rest of the country don't know about it won't hurt 'em any." He stood up, plainly eager to do his part. "How'll we git him down?" he asked, not because he did not know, but obeying an impulse toward speech that would make the thing less horrible.

"I can carry him, all right. Shelt, you look after the girl. You better stay here and kinda keep a lookout. And if Mary —the squaw—shows up, don't try to tell her anything about it. I'll handle her. She ain't right in her mind and she packs a knife. She might—" He did not feel that it was necessary to finish that sentence.

Shelton stood sober-eyed and watched Burney gather into his huge arms that monstrous form of a man and go staggering to the edge of the rock rim. He watched him part the bushes in a certain place with one hand, pause a minute there to make sure of his footing, and go down slowly, surely, like a man feeling his way down a crude stairway, bearing the limp Thing with the frozen snarl on its brutish face. Without a word, Spider followed him down out of sight.

When the strange, outlandish funeral procession had gone, Shelton turned and knelt beside Vida and began to chafe her little, sunburned hands pityingly, tenderly, and to watch her face for the first quiver of an eyelash that would tell how close she was to returning consciousness.

CHAPTER TWENTY-EIGHT

NO TROUBLE AT ALL

A ND so you see, Vida," Shelton's nice voice summed up the tale he had been telling her, "the whole thing was just an unfortunate circumstance which really was nobody's fault. You can't call a creature like that responsible for what he did. I don't suppose he had as much brain as the average animal. Because they do live according to certain animal laws which grow out of their instincts—and he—or it, I guess you'd say—wasn't even a normal animal."

"Who killed him?" Vida shivered at the memory of her horror. "Did Burney?"

"N-no—you see, he was killing Burney. He'd—well, he had gotten his fingers on Burney's throat, so—"

"Spider wasn't close enough. He was away down the other cañon. I saw him get off his horse and run, but he couldn't possibly have got here in time."

Shelton's face whitened. "Well—I was here, you see. I—shot him, Vida. I had to do it. He was killing Burney."

"You!" Vida sat up and stared at him as though she had never really seen him before. Which perhaps she hadn't. Not as he really was. "Why, I didn't think a tenderfoot—"

The blood rushed back into Shelton's face, and there was a snap in his eyes and in his voice when he retorted. "A tenderfoot out here may be pretty close to human, back where he came from. As a matter of fact, Spider or any of the rest of them would be pretty much of a side show back in New Jersey, you know." His jaw looked harder, somehow, and stronger. "We've had some pretty tough propositions to handle, in my home town, as it happens, and I usually managed to get myself right in the middle of them. That," he confessed shamefacedly, "is one reason why they shipped me out here. They were afraid I'd get myself killed. Dad said I'd find things much less exciting out West. I haven't, though," he finished naively. "The folks are going to be surprised when I write and tell them all that has happened in two weeks."

Vida's face was turned away from him but her voice was different when she spoke. "I'm glad it was you. Now they can't belittle you just because you're—"

"Green?"

"Not that so much. Handsome," said Vida reluctantly and immediately changed the subject. "I can't see why Burney permitted such a monstrosity to go around killing—"

With a sigh of relief, Shelton took up the defense. "Burney wasn't to blame, Vida. He said the—monstrosity—had always been harmless until he started killing your father's sheep. And he went to Pocatello to see what could be done

152

about it. A brain operation seemed to be his chief solution; or an institution. Only he said it would be too cruel to cage him up in an asylum.

"Burney's a fine man, Vida. He's big-hearted, as well as big-bodied. I wish you'd try and like him. He isn't to blame for that idiot thing. If you'd heard him talk—about how he feels he's looked upon as something queer, anyway, and if it were known he had a half-brother like that—Oh, say! Let's just forget that relationship, shall we? It was an accident, anyway. It made me choke up, when Burney said he felt shut off from folks. I wish you could like him, Vida, and—and let him see you do."

"My foot hurts terribly," Vida parried the tacit request and groaned a little. She moved her head restlessly in the crook of Shelton's arm, where it had been resting when she came to herself. "I stepped in a hole when I was running and gave it a pretty bad twist, I'm afraid. He—It—was coming right at me when I fell. I heard Burney yell, too, but I thought it was he who was chasing me and I never looked back. I never dreamed there were two of them. I'm glad the Thing is dead. Aren't you?"

"I'm—thankful it can't do any more harm or disgrace Burney," Shelton stated carefully and pressed his lips together. But something else was in his mind. He bent his handsome head and looked at the girl until she averted her face again.

"You—you saved my life," she said, almost whispering.

"Oh, no. I tried to get here in time, but I didn't. It was Burney who saved your life. You must thank him for that."

"But if he had killed Burney, he'd have—"

"I—I'd rather not talk about that," said Shelton stiffly. His face had gone white again. "I'd rather forget it altogether, if I could. I just want you to remember that you owe Burney your life and I hope you'll be good to him, Vida. Try and not let him see he's—well, strange and different. He wants to be like other folks, I guess. He acts offish and strange because he's ashamed of being so big. Just like—" he gulped and blushed—"just like me and my looks. I learned to fight for the simple reason that I wanted to lick every man who called me pretty." He gave an embarrassed laugh. "I just about broke them of the habit, back in Trenton."

153

"Why, you're—" She didn't finish. Shelton had his hand over her mouth so she couldn't.

"You'll have to get back to camp so that foot can be attended to," he said briskly, as if he had relieved his mind of some load. "Where's your horse, Vida? I'll go bring him up here. I can, by leading him up the point, there."

"Oh!" Vida shuddered in his arms. "It killed my pony. Just like the sheep."

"Oh, say! But that's too bad! We'll have to say he fell and broke his neck or something, won't we? Spider will know what could happen to a horse out here. And don't you think that had better account for your sprained ankle too? Horses do fall and hurt their riders—or is that just another one of the fellows' jokes?"

"It's no joke when it happens," Vida laughed ruefully.

"You won't be afraid, will you, Vida? If any one comes, it will only be Spider or Burney." Shelton eased her gently back against a rock and stood up. "I won't be gone any longer than is absolutely necessary. You aren't nervous about staying here alone, are you?"

Vida was but she lacked the courage to admit it. Instead, she smiled up at Shelton in a way that brought his heart leaping in his chest. He made one impulsive movement as if he were going to kneel and take her in his arms again—Vida thought he was going to and blushed—but he didn't quite dare. Not at that precise moment.

Still, he was bold enough. He stooped and kissed her full on the mouth that had tempted him so many times.

The minutes slipped by them unheeded after that. There was so much to say, even though he did not quite reach the point of asking an extremely vital question. "Say, you've got all the cowboys skinned for nerve," he declared, his arms around her at last. And he whispered something else not meant to be overheard even by the traditional little bird that tells everything.

"If Burney and Spider come back, tell them I've gone after my horse. Or I suppose Burney could help you down to where old Dutch is standing—you aren't really afraid of Burney, are you?"

"No," lied Vida in a small voice, "of course I'm not."

154

"You mustn't be. Burney's a prince. I'd like to carry you down in my arms, but it's pretty steep, and—I admit it might not be so comfortable for you. And I really think the sooner you get started for home, the better."

"I think so too."

"We've really got to think of Burney, you know. And if we're going to keep this thing quiet, I should think the sooner we all get away from here, the better it will be for all concerned. So if he comes, you'd better let him help you. In any case, I'll get old Dutch back down the bluff where you could ride him safely, and then, if you haven't shown up on the rim by that time, I'll bring him on around the point. You'll be able to see me, in any case. And Burney could take you down the point to meet me, if I've started on. That way," he finished cheerfully, "we won't be wasting any time waiting for them."

Still he didn't go, but held her close, hating to leave her even for a few minutes, after the terrors of the past hour. "You do like me, don't you?" he whispered close to her cheek. "Even if I am a tenderfoot?"

For answer Vida held him tight. But it was not altogether love that strengthened her clasp. She was afraid; horribly afraid. But she was more afraid that Shelton would suspect her fear and love her less because of it. So she forced herself to laugh a little, and she reached up a brown hand and straightened his hat and pinched his ear.

"I wish my foot didn't hurt so—I'd go with you," she said. "Hurry up, won't you? I'm not afraid of Burney, but I'm not in love with—*him*." She placed an artful emphasis upon the last word, so that Shelton would grudge every minute that separated them. And in this manner did Vida prove herself wholly feminine in spite of her overwrought emotions.

"Go on," she commanded him tenderly, "and don't be such a big silly. But hurry back, Shep, if you don't want me to change my mind about—liking you."

He took the "Shep" with a grin and he went because he wanted to help Burney out of his trouble. He was rather dazed yet, what with this miracle of Vida's love that had come to him so unexpectedly, and the amazing solution of the mystery that had grown so sinister. He looked back frequently while he was yet on the ridge, just to assure himself that Vida was really there.

As for Vida, she watched Shelton out of sight with sinking spirits. She was afraid, up there on the hilltop alone; horribly afraid. Her foot pained her dreadfully, now she had time to think about it, and she was thirsty. Her head throbbed, though she knew she was lucky to get off so lightly. But most of all she dreaded Burney's return. It was foolish, but one's nervous system does not reason or adjust itself automatically to changed conditions, and she had been so certain that it was Burney who was chasing her up the bluff—

She heard a rock kicked loose somewhere behind her and she turned sick with a fresh terror. She heard him coming heavily toward where she lay, his great feet crunching the gravelly soil like the tread of a horse. She shut her eyes; and then, when she felt that he was standing close beside her, she opened them wide and stared up at him.

There he was, towering miles above her—or so her overwrought nerves pictured him—and his little, twinkling eyes were fixed anxiously upon her face. He had something in his hands and while she stared at him she saw his face redden with embarrassment. It had been pale and drawn.

"I brought up some water from a spring down there," he said: "I thought maybe you'd like a drink."

"Oh, thanks!" Vida reached up for the leaky old tomato can which he carried in one hand. She had never dreamed of thanking Burney for anything.

"Where's Shelt?" he asked.

Vida took a last deep swallow and set down the can. In an hour of friendly protestations, Burney could not have reassured her so much as he had done by that one thoughtful little act. Her eyes lost their fear and became almost friendly.

"He's gone to get his horse and bring him up the ridge," she explained, "unless we meet him down below first."

"Well, that's a good idea. We'll go on down, then." Burney stood fifteen feet away from her and he spoke with a timid hesitation oddly at variance with his hugeness.

Vida waited. "I thought Shelton said Spider was with you."

"He was, but I showed him a way out of the cave into

156

the other gulch where he left his horse. He's going on back to the ranch."

Vida eyed him queerly. It began to dawn upon her that Alec Burney was actually timid with her. "I stepped in a hole and gave my foot a twist," she informed him, with an amused quirk of the lips. "I—I can't walk."

"Oh, that's too bad." Burney shifted his weight to the other foot, looking for all the world like a big, bashful boy.

Vida watched him covertly. "Shelton offered to carry me down, but he was afraid maybe he might drop me."

"Oh, did he?" Burney was already perspiring.

"He said maybe you wouldn't mind—helping me—a little." Vida reached down and felt her injured foot.

"Oh, I—I'll be glad to—help—" From collar to hatband Burney was purple with confusion.

"I'm afraid you'll have to carry me." Vida blushed a little herself, but her lips still had the amused half-smile. "If it wouldn't be—too much trouble," she added.

"Oh, no trouble at all—don't mention it! I—I hope we can—be friends, Miss Williams," he stammered.

"My name is Vida, and there's no use hashing things all over again. I'm really not so bad when you get to know me. You'll have to be careful not to joggle my foot—"

Not much of a reconciliation, so far as words went, but Burney's face lighted in a way that transformed his face.

Did you ever see a man take a butterfly from his net with almost a caressing carefulness, so as not to brush the bloom from its wings? Just so gently did Burney lift her into his arms and carry her down the bluff.

Vida spoke but once when he had carried her with safe gentleness down the steepest ledge. "It must be wonderful to be so strong," she said. "I'm like all the men in the country, I'm just simply jealous at the easy way you do things. They'd all give their eyeteeth to be as big as you are."

Burney did not answer her, but his eyes shone with gratitude and a shy pleasure.

CHAPTER TWENTY-NINE

SHELTON WRITES TO THE FOLKS

SHELTON sat in the bunk house that evening, writing at one end of the table while Spooky thumbed his deck of cards and glowered at his spread of Mexican solitaire at the other end. Between them stood the lamp, its chimney fogged with dust and smoke yet casting a yellow glow upon the deep wave in Shelton C. Sherman's yellow blond hair.

Between plays, while he shuffled the deck without knowing what his fingers were about, Spooky watched Shep's pen curiously, even tried to read the writing upside down. Then his eyes would lift to watch Shep's face from under his shaggy brows, his own face a study in affectionate impatience and a disgruntled kind of concern. Amazement would have been added, had he succeeded in reading what that tireless gold fountain pen inscribed in its interminable travels across ten full pages.

Things were written there which Spooky never dreamed of as fact, yet they were true as Shelton C. Sherman could set down the truth. For instance, the fifth page started off:

—marry me, and I'm sure you and dad would love her if you could know her as I do. I'd bring her back on our honeymoon, only she can't very well leave her father now that her uncle is dead. Her father is a sheep man, as it is called out here. He owns vast numbers of sheep and Vida is his business manager, so you see he can't get along without her very well, until he can find some one to take her place. Really she is a wonder, mom—rides and shoots and cooks and all that and is a perfect lady too.

That was one place where the pen was hung up for a good ten minutes while Shelton gnawed a knuckle and wondered just how his mother would interpret the word "lady." He decided to say nothing about her coming over to the Sunbeam and threatening to shoot Burney that time. It would be hard to make his folks understand how a "lady" could do a thing like that.

You thought it might be a good thing if I would take an interest in cattle raising or something, dad, and settle down. Well I have decided to go into sheep, as the saying is out here. That money in trust, you will know what I mean, the money Aunt Mary left, well I want to take that and buy an interest in Mr. Williams' sheep business. It is a good proposition and he will let me have a half interest in his sheep. So there is no reason why we can't get married right away, as Vida's father is short-handed, as he calls it, and Vida and I can take over the ewes and lambs that her uncle Jake was in charge of when he died. So if you will attend to the details of getting my money sent out here to me, dad, you can send it in care of Alec Burney at the Stockman's Bank in Pocatello; and get it there right away, because I am anxious to get married and settle down in these wide open spaces. We will have a couple of herders for the sheep and buy more dogs, as two dogs died by accident lately and we are short of dogs. Vida is a fine little cook and it is a very healthy life out here and I am sure you would approve of my decision if you could look the proposition over. Burney asked me to go in with him, and if there is enough coming to me so I can do it, I would like to put a little money into his business; that will not be putting all the eggs in one basket, as the saying goes. But if not, I will invest it all in sheep and stay with it and make good with the sweetest little girl in the world and the smartest and bravest. I say brave because I call it brave to live out here in these open spaces with only her father for company, and not complain any more than she has done. She is a wonderful girl, mom, and I want you to know her some day and love her as I do, only not the same way, of course—

"For the Lordy sake, Shep, what you writin'? A *book?*" asked Spooky just then, sweeping the cards together with his palm and speaking in a tone of deep disgust. The swift traveling of that pen had gotten on his nerves, especially since he could not see what was written.

"Honest to gollies, I should think the hind side of a picture postcard would hold all that happens in this darned desert. You tellin' about the spook?"

"Yes, and how I mean to exorcise it," Shelton retorted, adding, "Your aff. son, Shelt" at the bottom of the last page and making a bulky fold of the letter.

"Hunh. It'll exercise *you*, if you don't keep outa them hills," grunted Spooky. "What all did yuh tell 'em? Say anything about how Spider's been shinin' up to yore girl? You wanta look out, Shep. Spider's took to shavin' most as often as what you do, and that shore means he's takin' down his loop for some girl. That there Williams girl—"

"You go to hell," said Spider in a vicious tone and got up and went outside.

"Yes, please do so," Shelton urged him crisply. "And be just a bit careful how you speak of my future wife, will you."

Breed Jim gave a snort and almost swallowed his cud. And Spooky sank back against the wall and stared at Shelton, pop-eyed.

"Well, I'm damned!" he gasped.

Shelton C. Sherman did not hear him. He had just thought of something else and was adding a hasty postscript:

Mom, please pick me out a nice diamond ring and send it at once. About the size of an ordinary girl's little finger. Vida has an awfully small hand, love—Shelt.

THE END

Bertha Muzzy Bower, born in Cleveland, Minnesota, in 1871, was the first woman to make a career of writing Western fiction and remains one of the most widely known, having written nearly seventy novels. She became familiar with cowboys and ranch life at sixteen when her family moved to the Big Sandy area of Montana. She was nearly thirty and mother of three before she began writing under the surname of the first of her three husbands. Her first novel, *Chip, of the Flying U,* was initially published as a serial in 1904 and was an immediate success. Bower went on to write more books, fourteen in all, about the Flying U, one of the best being the short story collection, *The Happy Family.* In 1933 she turned to stories set prior to the events described in *Chip, of the Flying U. The Whoop-up* actually begins this saga, recounting Chip Bennett's arrival in Montana and at the Flying U. Much of the appeal of this saga is due to Bower's use of humor, the strong sense of loyalty and family depicted among her characters, as well as the authentic quality of her cowboys. She herself was a maverick who experimented with the Western story, introducing modern technologies and raising unusual social concerns—such as aeroplanes in *Skyrider* or divorce in *Lonesome Land.* She was sensitive to the lives of women on the frontier and created some extraordinary female characters, notably in Vada Williams in *The Haunted Hills*, Georgie Howard in *Good Indian,* Helen in *The Bellehelen Mine,* and Mary Allison in *Trouble Rides the Wind*, another early Chip Bennett story. She was also able to write Western novels memorable for the characterization of setting and dramatization of nature, such as *Van Patten* or *The Swallowfork Bulls.*